Buzz

Night Howler's MC
New Orleans
Book 1

By: Marissa Ann

Warning:
Credits:
Cover Design by: Francessca PR & Designs
Editor: Rachel Goldman
Blurb: Melissa Mitchell

ASIN:
ISBN-13: 978-1-7365798-1-7

Author's Note

Thanks to all my fans for your patience for new releases. You guys ROCK!

Hope you enjoy this fresh start of a new series from a few characters you have already met. If you want to keep up to date on what I have going on, look to the back of this book with how you can contact me.

Prologue
Buzz

Several years ago, my little sister was raped and murdered. Her killer was never caught. She had been emailing a guy she had met in an online chat room. Even though the authorities had his name he used online, every lead came to a dead end. It didn't stop me from continuing the search.

A few weeks ago I caught a break. Another programmer I knew from when I was still in the service stumbled across the same name with a different unique IP address that constantly bounces around making it almost impossible to follow.

However, follow it I did and where it winds up leading me has me second guessing what I am planning.

I'll take something from him. His beautiful sister Markayla. But we don't hurt innocents. I will protect her as best I can. I plan on her step brother paying for what he did to my sister with his own blood. What I don't plan for is falling hard for my enemy's sister.

Markayla

Even after all of these years I can't believe my mother was stupid enough to fall for my step father. I have never doubted he had something to do with her disappearance. I've just never been able to prove it.

You would think that with her gone, I'd be free of the Marcus family. Unfortunately for me, my step father adopted me when he married my mother.

My step brother absolutely hates me and I am certain that our Papa is the only one keeping him from doing whatever he wants to me.

The look I see in his eyes any time I run into him while I am out with friends or a date scares me to my core. I refuse to let him know just how scared of him I really am.

If anything ever happens to Papa or I become expendable in his eyes, I will need to run and run fast. Getting away before he gives me to Joe to do whatever he wants with me, will take a miracle.

Chapter 1
Markayla

The last six months of my life have been a living hell. Papa Tony left out of the country on business leaving Joey, my adopted step-brother essentially in charge of the family business here in New Orleans.

He's the reason I now rarely sleep. He and his cronies forced me to move out of my apartment and back into the main house surrounded by guards. According to him, Papa Tony demanded it and no one says no to Papa Tony. Not even me.

Papa Tony was always a hard man that never really showed any type of affection for anyone. I rarely ever saw him hold my mothers hand. I asked her about it once; she just said he had very good reasons as to why. Sounded stupid and cryptic if you asked me.

When Joey forced me back into the main house, he had his guards take away my phone as well as my computer. While I never saw my phone again, I stumbled across a computer that I thought was mine but looking at it now, I know that it isn't.

For a couple weeks now my guards that are always shadowing me have become lax in their duties by leaving me unattended at a local coffee shop that I go to daily.

I've purposely cultivated my daily routine to be as boring as humanly possible in hopes that they would back off a little so that I can make plans to get as far away from here as I can.

There are a lot of files on this computer that I found that I want to break the encryption to get into them. They have to be truly important to have such sophisticated code hiding them. Hopefully something that I can take to the authorities to put Joey behind bars forever. The shithead truly scares me.

I have to find a way to break this code before they figure out this computer is missing. I use the cafe's free wifi to look for someone on the dark web that might help me. This morning there is an encrypted message that I can easily get into that was sent to my email.

Someone responded to my inquiry about this specific code. All they sent was an address with a time to be there. Hoping that I am doing the right thing and not about to get caught, I close the computer to scan the area to see where the guards are at.

Getting up, I head towards the restrooms knowing the ladies room has a window just big enough that I can crawl out. From there, I can grab a cab several streets from here before they realize that I'm gone.

Buzz

Since tracking down the computer that is connected to my sisters' murder, I've figured out that the girl that has it couldn't possibly be connected directly. She looks way too innocent for one thing plus we started tracking her on the web.

Apparently she's a programmer but doesn't have the same skill set that I do. Not many have those skills though. Geniuses aren't born every day after all. Does that make me conceited? Probably but even I know that I'm super smart. It's just facts.

When she advertised within a group on the dark web looking for a hacker that could read a specific code, I jumped on it fast not wanting another to get in my way. After answering her directly, I went in and erased any trace of what she had posted so that it could not be traced.

I left my email super cryptic just naming a place within the park with a time to meet me. It's still fairly public but we can hide in plain sight while watching who comes or goes.

I've seen the goons that are normally with her at the cafe. It's why I've been unable to just snatch her away to a place where I could question her without a lot of fuss.

Basically I didn't want to call up Skeeter, the President of my club, to tell him we needed a cleanup of bodies on Main Street. He just might kill me for that one. I certainly have no qualms about getting bloody as long as they aren't innocent like my sweet little sister was.

She was a beautiful girl. So sweet and bright, she was everything I wasn't. She viewed the world around her like it was full of miracles and wonders yet to be explored. I was always trying to warn her of the evils of the world while she would just laugh and say that I was so cynical.

She wanted to be a doctor and would have been amazing at it if her life hadn't been cut short because of some dickhead that just wanted to snuff her out as if she didn't ever exist.

I plan to snuff out the mother fucker that took her from me. The only shining light I ever had in my life. Whoever he is, I will cut off his testicles and feed them to him after he watches me cook them over an open fire like marshmallows.

Getting to the meeting spot ahead of time, I pick a bench under a tree that gives me a view of every angle of the park.

An hour later I watch as she comes across the park from the East entrance. She's not spotted me yet but I can see every inch of her. Before, I had never really paid attention to what she looked like but as I watch her now, my eyes seem to take over scanning her from head to feet.

My body seems to take notice of her shapely legs that lead up to an hourglass figure with nice breasts. She's the exact type that I would normally go for a fast fuck with her legs above both of our heads.

Fuck! I need to get laid and stop gawking at her like this! I think to myself as I adjust myself behind my zipper.

She gets to the statue that is a few feet away looking around her until her eyes land on me. At first she looks away before looking back again.

"Um, I'm Markayla. Are you the guy I'm supposed to meet?" She asks tentatively.

"Yeah. Name is Buzz. You said you had an encryption you didn't know how to break. You have it with you?" I ask as I scan the area behind her for the guards that are normally tailing her. Not seeing them yet, I look back at her.

"It's in my backpack but look, we need to go somewhere else. It's possible I may be followed." She looks behind her again. I notice she looks scared.

She should be if what I think is on that computer is really on there. Her mentioning wanting to go somewhere else will make this easier for me. I had thought I would have to lie or even physically take her against her will.

"I have a place we can go. My computers are there that I'll need to help me break the code anyway." I stand up and start walking towards a different exit than the one she came through. Looking back, I see that she finally starts to follow me.

Markayla

I study Buzz as I follow him out of the park. He's nothing like I had expected. I thought he would be some geeky looking guy, skinny and with glasses. But he's the opposite of all those things.

The man is hotness with legs coupled with those tattoos crawling up his arms. Everything about him screams bad boy and I've never been too impressed with the bad boy types. This one though is drool worthy.

"Where are we going exactly?" I finally ask as we leave the busier streets behind. Realizing that I will be alone with this man, hot or not, he could potentially be dangerous.

"You don't want to be followed right? I'm parked just around this corner, and then we'll take the streets that don't have cameras to my apartment where my computers are."

"Why would you know which streets have cameras?" I ask with surprise.

"I'm a hacker. I don't want anyone to be able to track my movements." His explanation seems legitimate although I am still uncertain if I am doing the right thing.

It has to be the right thing. I think to myself as we reach his vehicle. It's an SUV with dark tinted windows. Getting into the passenger side, I put on my seat belt as we pull away from the curb.

I watch as we head farther outside of the city limits to the warehouse districts. Neither of us saying a word as the time slowly drags by. It only takes us around thirty minutes when we pull up to a warehouse surrounded by a gate that opens automatically as we pull up.

"This is where you live?" I ask, getting out of the vehicle looking up at the building in front of us.

"Yes. It doesn't look like much from out here but I completely renovated the inside when I bought the place. Come on, I'll show you." He heads toward the front door expecting me to follow.

I look back at the gate and realize that I am completely locked in. To get out, he would have to open the gate for me. Trying not to let my brain go crazy with thoughts of being murdered by this super hot guy, I follow him inside.

Stepping through the door, I am floored with how updated it is. It's truly beautiful with all hardwood flooring and modern furniture. It's just as beautiful as many of the mansions my family has lived in or visited over the years.

"This is beautiful." I breathe out looking all around.

"Thanks. The computer room is this way." He points ahead of him, waiting for me to follow.

Walking into the room he indicated, it is covered with computers and monitors as well as other gadgets I don't know the name of.

On one wall, there's dozens of surveillance feeds playing across the screens. It's as if he is monitoring the entire city from this one little room.

Buzz

"If you'll hand it to me now, I'll get started on breaking through the code." I hold my hand out waiting for her to hand me the computer from her backpack.

Once she hands it to me, I begin connecting it to all of my own computers to begin downloading my own software that will help to get past the encryptions and firewalls.

"How long will it take?" She asks as she watches me work.

"It's hard to say really. It depends on a lot of different factors. It could take hours, days or even weeks. If it can be cracked though, I'm the only guy that can do it."

"What makes you so sure that you can?" She puts one hand on her hip and I'm again struck with how beautiful she really is.

"Because I'm the best." I state matter of factly.

"Little full of yourself aren't you?" She rolls her eyes.

"No. I'm just honest." I turn away from her and begin to do what I do best.

I listen as she moves around the room before sitting down on the couch against the wall. She's quiet for a little while before she stands up yet again.

"Look, I really need to get back before anyone realizes that I'm gone." She says nervously, looking at the time on her phone.

"You can't." I say simply.

"I can't what?" She looks at me with confusion.

"Leave." The one word answer seems to make her go completely still.

"You can't stop me." She whispers, her hand slipping down inside of her purse.

Her eyes go wide at the realization that the pepper spray she had inside is no longer there. I lifted it out while she was occupied watching out the window of the car on the way here.

Getting up, I stalk towards her. With each step forward she takes a step back until I have her cornered against the wall behind her only stopping less than a foot from her.

"What is it that you want?" She says, trying to stare me down.

"Are you close to your brother?" I ask, still staring right at her.

"He's not my brother!" She says through gritted teeth.

"You really have no idea just what the hell you have found yourself in the middle of, do you?" I inch closer to her, watching as her eyes widen.

"And you do?" She crosses her arms over her chest which draws my eyes involuntarily to the orbs I am sure I would love to play with for a while.

When she notices where my eyes went, she quickly drops her arms and her eyes turn to slits.

"My face is up here jackass." She grumbles out.

I grin at her in response.

"I know more than you think about your brother's business. I'm going to take a guess here that you suspect something but don't actually know anything." I raise my brow at her.

"Something like that." She waits to see what I'll say next.

"Look, for now just watch a movie or something while I break the code into the computer. I'll order take out. When it gets here, I'll try to explain what I know so far." I watch as she begins walking around the room looking at the few pictures I have scattered around.

She stops at the one of my sister and me. It's the last one taken of the two of us before she was killed. The last club BBQ we attended. Her smiling face that day is how I prefer to remember her.

"Who is this girl?" Markayla looks over at me.

"My sister, Melody. She died a few years ago." I look away, back towards my computers.

"Are you sure she's dead?" Her question catches me off guard and I turn back to her.

"Of course I'm sure! Why wouldn't I be? I had to look at her burned body!" I growl at her.

"Look, I don't mean to upset you. It's just that she looks exactly like a girl that comes to the dinner parties Joey has for his creepy friends. She's always with that asshole Pecker Pete." She says.

"Pecker Pete?" I ask with a grin.

"It's my nickname for him, when he's not around of course." She smiles back, lifting her shoulder.

"Just think about it, Buzz. These guys Joey runs with are some of the upper crust of society. Creeps of course but they have major money. Enough to buy off cops and judges. I don't want you to get your hopes up but I swear to God, she looks just like her." She says.

She does have a point and it's not like I don't know about crooked politicians or cops. I'm in a motorcycle club that has been on both sides of the law at one point or another.

"Let's say this is all true and it's her. How would we find this Pecker Pete as you call him?" I ask.

My heart hammers. I'm scared to get my hopes up but just the thought of the burned body I identified as my sister, twists my stomach.

Could she really be alive? If she is alive why hasn't she contacted me? Where has she been? All these questions rush through my head but I need to focus on the computer. That's where I'll get my answers.

"I'm hoping for your sake it's on that blasted computer because if it's not, then that means either getting our hands on Joey or calling my cousin." Her face scrunches up at the thought.

"Is your cousin in on this as well?" I ask, moving back to my chair in front of the computer.

"I doubt it. But he's definitely loyal to Papa Tony." She answers.

"And your father? Where does he fit in here?" I look up at her for an answer.

"He's not my father. Not my real father anyway. I'm not sure who it is. My mom never said. I'm not sure what Papa Tony knows about any of this. At first I thought there was no way that he couldn't know that something was going on, now I'm not so sure.

He left town more than a year ago and I've not heard from him. Not that I would expect to. He never seemed to like me." She says it like it doesn't matter but her eyes betray the hurt she feels deep inside.

"We will figure it all out." I say although it feels inadequate considering everything.

"I have one question. Why are you willing to help me?" She turns her full attention back to me.

"As I said, I know you are innocent in all of this. You shouldn't have to pay for the sins of your family, blood or not." I state simply, turning back to my computer.

Chapter 2
Markayla

For some reason I believe everything Buzz has told me so far. My gut feeling is that I can trust him, so I'm going with it.

He said that for up to so many miles around his home he has some sort of gadget that scrambles our phones so that they can't be traced back here to where we are.

Not that I have anyone that I would want to call. Papa Tony is out of the country and I'm still not yet convinced that I can trust him. With mom dead, I'm all alone.

There is my cousin, Baratta but I don't know if he would protect me from the family or not. He works for them and is completely loyal. We were always close though. Would he save me even if the person wanting me gone was Papa Tony? I wouldn't want to put it to a test.

Buzz ordered takeout. He had it delivered to the front gate and asked me to stay inside, so nobody would see me. We weren't followed but Joey has people everywhere.

We ate mostly in silence. I don't mind really, I never could stand being around people who wanted to spend every waking moment constantly talking.

Guess that's why I loved programming so much even though I'm not hacker material. I do, however, love writing programs or creating systems specifically for certain businesses to keep track of their expenses.

"If you want to rest, the last door on the right is the guest bedroom. The bathroom is across the hall." Buzz says from his computer without turning around.

"Thanks." I say but he doesn't answer back.

Heading towards the bedroom, I decide that I could really use a shower before lying down on a clean bed. I don't have any clean clothes though.

Looking down at my clothes, I decide that since the bathroom is just across the hall I can just wrap the towel around me until I get into the bedroom with the door shut.

Walking into the bathroom, I'm surprised at the huge walk in shower with multiple shower heads. I grin just thinking about how amazing it will feel to have the hot water coming from all directions like a massage.

Buzz

Normally when I'm in my zone, nothing can distract me from the screens in front of me. But Markayla seems to be an exception.

I've noticed every single time she has moved even the slightest little bit. Knowing that she left to go get some rest I'm hopeful that I can concentrate more with her gone.

For several minutes, I'm doing great until I hear my shower turn on with the jet sprays. My mind immediately wonders what she looks like with soapy water running down her gorgeous body. I groan as I feel my cock spring to life.

I'm still sitting there staring off into space imagining her inviting me in when my phone rings. Looking down, I see it's a call from Skeeter, the president of my club.

"Thought you were going to call me with an update." He demands before I can even say hello.

"The girl is here." I say.

"Is she going to be a problem?" He asks quietly.

"She's willing to help." I answer.

"Good. From all the Intel about her as well as Joey, she's going to need our protection during all of this. One of the guys that was captured during the trafficking ring fiasco has been talking to our FBI contact Special Agent

Richards. According to him, Joey is completely in love with his adopted sister." Skeeter says.

"I'm pretty sure she doesn't feel the same way." I state, looking down the hall where I still hear the water running.

"Agent Richards also heard from Tony Marcus." He lays that bombshell down quickly.

"Why would he call an FBI agent?" I growl through the phone.

"He's been down in South America chasing a lead on his presumed dead wife. Agent Richards didn't give me the full details but it sounded like she's not dead after all and Joey has something to do with it. He called Richards because he has been unable to get in touch with his daughter and he doesn't have anyone here he trusts to figure out why." Skeeter explains.

"I'm not sure she is convinced that he isn't involved. He's not even her real father." I lean against the wall holding the phone to my ear.

"Oh, but he is." Skeeter chuckles.

"What do you mean?" I push away from the wall.

"According to him, he was always afraid of his enemies using her against him. So he and his wife came up with the plan to pretend that she was born from a different father. They never named anyone as her father, but they were so convincing that even she doesn't know the truth." Skeeter answers quickly as I hear someone walk into his office.

"There's no fucking way I'm telling her that." I grit through the phone.

"You won't have to. Just keep her safe for now. Word has already spread on the street that Joey is looking for her. Call if you get anything on the computer." He says hanging up before I can reply.

I'm sticking my phone in my back pocket when the bathroom door opens. I can't believe my eyes when I watch her walk out in nothing but a towel that barely covers her. She jumps a little when she notices me in the hallway.

"You scared me. I thought you'd be busy with your computers." One hand holds her towel in front just above her breasts.

It's her legs though that are currently catching my attention. Fuck, she's got legs that look more than capable of wrapping around me to hold on as I pump into her against the closest wall.

I realize that I have been staring the whole time without saying a word. Looking back up at her face, I can see that her eyes show interest. Such responsive eyes. I'd love to see them while she comes on my face. I grin at the thought.

"I was just heading to my room for a few hours." I hear the growl in my voice the same time she does, her eyes widen and her breathing kicks up. Walking towards her, I stop only a breath away from her.

"Get anything on the computer?" She asks breathily, looking up into my eyes.

I take a deep breath, smelling my soap on her. My cock once again turns to iron.

"Not yet." I say.

"Were you just sniffing me?" She asks in an affronted way.

"My soap smells good on you. I wonder what else of mine would smell good on your body." I lean in, whispering in her ear.

I smile wondering if she would drop the towel and let me see if her nipples tightened up at the thought I just placed into her head.

"I'll see you in the morning." She quickly says, going around me into the bedroom, closing the door behind her.

Markayla

After closing the door behind me, I sit down on the bed while my heart beats like crazy. I've never had a man to affect me as easily as Buzz seems to do.

Just a look, a small whisper from him, has my entire body humming in anticipation. Goosebumps pop up all over my skin just thinking about his eyes.

Pulling the covers back on the bed, I climb in after throwing the towel over the chair next to the bed.

The sheets are super soft against my skin. I'm pretty sure they are real silk. The way they feel rubbing against me does nothing to alleviate the feelings Buzz induced.

My nipples tighten up even more as I slide further into the bed. I can't stop the sigh that escapes my lips.

Buzz's face pops into my head and I concentrate on the color of his eyes. My mind conjures an image of him between my thighs as he looks back at me. I'm instantly soaked, my face flaming at the thought of my juices leaking onto his bed.

I shouldn't be thinking of him like this so soon after meeting him. How will I be able to look at him in the morning while knowing what I was doing in his guest room to images in my head of him?

My hand slides down to my folds, covering my fingers in my wetness. As my fingers plunge into my slit while the pad of my hand hits my clit, all thoughts of being embarrassed in the morning fade as a new feeling takes over.

I'm so close to coming within seconds. I imagine him pinching my nipples as I ground myself further onto his tongue.

My orgasm explodes from my body and I bite my lips to hold back the groan that seems to come from deep within me.

"Damn." I whisper out loud a few minutes later when my heart returns to normal.

Cleaning myself off with the towel I left on the chair, I lay back down in the bed and fall asleep quickly.

Buzz

I wake in the middle of the night with my cock still just as hard as it was when Markayla came out of the shower.

Trying to ignore it, I roll over hoping it'll just go away but the pressure from the bed just has me imagining plunging deep into her while her legs are over my shoulders.

I can't take it any more as I reach down, squeezing my cock, giving it a few hard strokes. Closing my eyes, I think about her responsive eyes as my hand gets faster.

It doesn't take long before my balls tighten up with a warning that they are going to explode. My strokes get even more erratic as my mind thinks about having her up against the wall, legs held high with my arms as I go as deep as possible into her slick moist heat.

I can feel my orgasm but I just can't seem to get myself over the edge no matter how fast or hard I pump my cock with my hand. It's not until I remember how my name sounded coming from her lips that I explode into my hand with a hard growl.

I don't think I've ever come so hard in my life as I lay there, holding my now deflated cock in my hand unsure if I can even move yet.

Eventually I get up to clean myself up before crawling back into my bed. Hopefully

that will settle my cock for a little while although
I doubt it.

Why does this girl get such a reaction out
of me? I wonder as I finally drift back off to
sleep.

Chapter 3
Buzz

I wake up a few hours later to my phone beeping telling me to check the computers in my office. It's an indication that it has either cracked the code or has hit a firewall. Getting dressed quickly, I head to my office.

Looking at the screens I can see that it has managed to open the computer fully and is now downloading all the information onto a disk. It's a backup in case anything were to shut the system down without warning.

"Not so high tech after all." I mumble, smiling as I watch it work quickly.

It'll take a while to finish up it's processes so that I can begin looking through all the files. My body buzzes with anticipation and I'm unable to sit still.

That is how I got my road name all those years ago. When I'm hyped up, I buzz around like a bee that can't stay still.

Looking at my phone, I think about calling Skeeter but seeing the time, he'd probably ride over here to kick my ass. I don't know why others can't seem to function at four in the morning.

Skeeter was in the military like I was. While I kept up my habit of barely sleeping and getting up early, Skeeter likes his sleep.

I text one of the prospects instead, asking them to bring some clothes for Markayla. Hopefully I got the sizes correct. I'm sure she would appreciate something clean to wear.

After I send the text, I head into the kitchen to make some breakfast. I'm just finishing up my eggs when I hear Markayla walk down the hall.

Looking up, I see she's put the same clothes on and while her hair is a bit messy, she's still just as beautiful as she was yesterday.

"Want some breakfast?" I ask.

"Just coffee for now if you have it." She answers with a slight smile.

I look at her a second longer wondering about the look on her face. She almost looks embarrassed and I'm not sure why.

Handing her a coffee mug, I turn back to finish my eggs.

"Anything from the computer yet?" She asks after taking her first sip of coffee with a sigh.

"My system got access. It's now downloading all the information. After that, we can take our time going through all of it to see what we can find." I answer, taking a seat at the bar with my plate.

"It got in already? Wow. Did you design the system yourself?" She asks with curiosity.

I shake my head in answer, continuing to eat my breakfast. She stays quiet after that as if she knows I don't like to talk much.

I'm just getting up to rinse my plate when the front gate buzzer sounds. Looking at the screen in my office, I press a button letting the prospect in the gate.

"Someone here?" She asks and I look back at her quickly.

"I got someone to bring you some clothes. Stay right here, I'll be right back." I tell her, walking out the door.

"Hey man, I brought everything you asked for on the list." Ranger says, handing me a bag as well as a pack of smokes.

Setting the bag down on the step, I open the smokes, lighting one up with a deep drag.

"You okay? You don't usually smoke." Ranger looks at me with concern.

He and I have known each other for many years although he didn't come into the club until much later than I did. He knew my sister all those years ago and I honestly thought the two of them would be a thing eventually. He was just as devastated by her death as I was.

"Got some information that I'm trying to not let my hopes get up on." I look over at him.

"Something about Mel?" He guesses.

"Yeah. Markayla thinks that she might be alive." I say in a rush.

"How? We saw her body. They identified her at the morgue." He stands up straight with agitation.

"The morgue could have been paid off. Hell, we know that most officials can be paid off." Throwing the smoke down, I ground it under my boot.

"This is fucked up." Ranger says after we are both silent for a few minutes.

"Yeah. Because there's a chance she's been out there this whole time waiting to be saved. Instead, I gave up the second I saw the burned body." I sigh, rubbing my face hard.

"You can't beat yourself up over that. Hell, we both thought it was her. If there's a chance she's still out there, we have to find her." Ranger's voice becomes hard as steel.

"Yeah, and then kill every mother fucker that kept her from us." I growl.

Markayla

I watch Buzz from the monitors for a few minutes. I see the two of them sit on the front step, lighting up cigarettes.

Sitting down to wait for him to come back, I watch the computer system quickly downloading files.

I can't believe how many are on this damn thing as I watch them move quickly across the screen.

Eventually it looks like it's copying files of people. It's moving so quickly that I can't get a good look at the file before it moves on but I know each one has a picture attached to it.

I bet everything in my soul that Buzz's sister is in there somewhere. There's no way the girl I met was just a look alike. It was her and I feel it in my bones. I only wish that she had given some indication at the time that she was in trouble. I would have helped her.

She probably thought I was in on all of it. I grimace at the thought. I'm not built that way. I could never stand by as someone forced another woman into something she didn't want.

I finally hear the door open as Buzz comes back in.

"There's some clothes in this bag. Hopefully the fit will be okay." He mumbles, handing me the bag.

"Thanks. Um, I noticed it scanned through some files that looked like they had photos attached. It could be files of some of the women they've taken." I look up at him.

"It looks like it is almost done with the download. We'll see if we can find those files again when it finishes." He says calmly but his eyes show keen interest.

I can tell he wants to find his sister still alive. I hope for both of them that the girl I met is her and that she's still out there somewhere.

After going into the bedroom and changing into some fresh clothes that surprisingly fit perfectly, I find Buzz steadily working at his computer.

Taking a seat in the room I watch him for a while as he works but I start to get bored.

"Isn't there something I can help with? I may not be as good as you but I do know computers." I ask his back.

"Here. This one is connected into the system. Start looking for those files you mentioned. I need to step outside and call my President." He says.

"Your President?" I ask, unsure what he means.

"Yeah, of my club. Skeeter is the President." He answers.

"Oh, yeah, sure." I answer even though I'm still unsure exactly how a motorcycle club works. "You guys aren't into illegal stuff are you?" I ask before he walks out of the room.

"Not any more." He turns back with a quick grin before disappearing around the corner.

A few seconds later, I see him on the monitor standing on the front step pulling his phone up to his ear.

"What does he mean by not any more?" I ask out loud with a shake of my head.

Putting it out of my mind for now, I get to work on the computer. Hoping like hell I can find the girl that I know is his sister.

Buzz

"I got in. My system just finished downloading all the information." I say as soon as Skeeter picks up.

"Send a copy to Agent Richards but I want you to go through the files to see if we can finally shut down Joey's operation." Skeeter says.

"I plan to. There's something else." I say into the phone.

"What is it?" He asks, more alert from the tone of my voice.

"Mel might still be alive." I rush out.

"No fucking way. What makes you think it's a possibility?"

"Markayla saw a picture of Mel. That one from the last family barbeque. She swears she's seen a girl that could be her twin at one of the dinner parties, Joey likes to hold for his crooked cronies. The guy she was with, Markayla only knows him as Pete. She doesn't really know anything else about him." I explain, waiting to see if he thinks the idea is as crazy as my mind hopes it is.

Because the thought that I have left her out there to suffer from God knows what will kill what's left of me on the inside.

"You don't worry about anything else other than going through all those files. If there's a chance Mel is still out there, she is our top

priority. Fuck everything else!" Skeeter growls
through the phone.

"That's my plan." I say with strong
determination.

"Call me when we have something more
to go on. I'll tell all the guys here about these
new developments." He says before hanging up.

I sit on the steps a bit longer, finishing
another cigarette. It's a nasty habit that I only do
when my mind is weighed heavily with other
shit. Mel would probably kick my ass to know
that I still smoke sometimes.

The image of her smiling face brings me a
few minutes of peace before I head back inside
to try to find my sister in all the files on my
computer. Hopefully, the universe brought
Markayla and that computer into my life for a
greater purpose. To find my sweet sister and
bring her home.

Markayla

We both have worked in silence since he came back from talking to his president. There are so many files on this computer it is insane.

Finally locating the files on various women sometime around lunch, we both steadily work our way through them trying to connect them with missing persons reports since none of them have the women's real name on them.

"We should take a break for a bit. We've been at it all day." Buzz says, standing up from his desk.

"What time is it?" I ask, looking up at him.

"Just after seven." He answers, walking out the door.

Following him into the kitchen, I take a seat at the bar as I watch him grab us both some drinks from the fridge.

"So what are we eating?" I ask with a smile.

"How about a pizza and a salad? I can call that place just around the corner." He asks from his propped up position against the counter.

"Other than breakfast, don't you ever cook?" I ask seriously.

"I'm single." He shrugs. "What's the point in cooking just for myself?" His grin is too sexy.

"For one, it's better for you. There's no telling how many arteries you have clogged." I state, looking him over from head to toe.

Big mistake because his body is toned to perfection. He's probably able to eat anything that doesn't eat him first without ever gaining a pound.

Thinking about him eating has my mind remembering my thoughts last night of having him between my thighs.

Looking up into his eyes, I just know he can guess where my thoughts strayed to judging by the now even bigger grin on his face.

"I'll call in our order. Why not find us something to watch on the TV while we eat." He says the last word slowly, watching me with keen eyes. I know my face has heated up and I quickly look away walking out of the room.

Hearing him chuckle behind me makes me roll my eyes. Damn my face for always betraying my thoughts.

Chapter 4
Markayla

We both must have fallen asleep during the movie and somehow wound up wrapped around each other.

The way he's laying with his face buried in my neck and breathing on my tender skin is wreaking havoc on my body.

Moving slightly, I try to get in a position where I can move off of him but his arms tense up when I do.

"Don't move. Just stay." I hear his voice whisper against me and I shiver.

I feel his lips gently kiss the pulse point on my neck, a groan escapes my lips.

"You are so beautiful." He whispers, kissing the shell of my ear as he pulls me tighter against his muscled body.

I can feel the hard length of him against the curve of my ass. Wanting more, I push further back into him.

His hand glides up the front of my body from my thigh, underneath my shirt. Not stopping until he has my left breast in his hand. Even through the material of my bra, there's no way he hasn't noticed the hard peaks of my nipples.

Still grinding into him, he gently pinches my hard nipple between his thumb and forefinger. It's like a shock to my system as it unleashes a dam inside of me. I can feel the slickness of myself between my thighs, my core throbbing for attention.

Rolling us until he is under me with my back still to his front giving him a better reach with both his hands as they push my bra up letting my breasts free for him to play with.

Still kissing my neck, he takes his time playing with my hard peaks until his hands glide down my stomach to open the clasp on my pants. Not wasting a second, his right hand goes straight to my throbbing core, coating his fingers with my juices.

"So fucking wet. You going to let me take you like this? Right here on this coach?" He growls into my ear as his fingers pinch my clit hard causing a moan. "Need the words, beautiful." He groans out himself as if barely restraining himself.

"Yes." I manage but just barely, needing him to settle the ache between my legs.

"Reese." He says, as he fumbles for what I believe is a condom from his wallet.

"What?" I ask in a daze.

"That's my name. The one I want to hear on your lips when you are coming on my cock." He growls as his cock springs free of his jeans as he pulls them down to his thighs

It is currently sticking out straight and I can see at least half of it sticking out from between my legs. I've never had a cock so big. I lick my lips in anticipation as he holds me up enough to slip the condom on.

Gliding his now sheathed cock back and forth through my folds coating himself with my wetness.

He has my legs pulled up with his heavily muscles arms and I know in this position he will go deeper than anyone ever has before.

Lifting me even more slightly, he lines the head of his cock up with my slit and slowly lowers me onto him.

It's a tight fit but he doesn't stop until he's all the way into the hilt. My eyes have already rolled to the back of my head from the way he fills me so completely.

"Oh fuck, you feel so good." He groans, easing out of me slightly to push back in.

He starts out slow but soon his rhythm picks up speed until all you can hear in the room are our own groans as skin slaps against skin.

"I'm going to come." I say a few minutes later but as soon as I speak he stops completely.

"No. You don't come until I say so, Markayla. Do you understand?" He asks and I shake my head until he's slowly moving again.

It's as if he has all the control of my body as it keeps me hanging with my orgasm just out of reach.

Pulling out, he lays me on the couch as he crawls over the top of me.

"I promised myself that you'd come on my face first while I watched those beautiful eyes of yours." He grins, pushing my legs up with his shoulders, his mouth only inches from my center.

Diving his tongue deep into me without warning. I yell out but he pulls his tongue back, latching onto my clit with his lips.

Very quickly he goes back and forth between diving his tongue into my core and sucking hard on my clit while his tongue vibrates against it.

My body winds up as tight as it can but still doesn't let go.

"Come for me Markayla." He growls, going back to work licking my folds.

That seems to release whatever lock was inside of me as I scream out his name with my eyes locked to his.

"Fucking beautiful." He whispers, crawling up my body the rest of the way, lining his still hard cock with my center once more.

He slams into me while the aftershocks of my orgasm are still running through me. My core is still tightening up in throbs that now feel wonderful with his hard length inside of me.

He sets a hard pace, slapping into me, hitting my clit with his pelvic bone each time his cock hits my secret spot on the inside.

Both his hands are buried in my hair, holding my face close to his as he keeps me in a deep kiss.

"Come again for me baby. Let me feel you let go." He whispers into my mouth.

The dam breaks again but this time so does his. We both come together, each of us saying the other's name until we are completely spent, covered in sweat on his couch.

Buzz

After leaving Markayla on the couch to go dispose of the condom, I come back to see that she has fallen asleep once again. Her gorgeous body on full display. I can feel my cock start to harden again.

This woman intrigues me which could be both good and bad. Good because there has never been another like her. Bad because she could prove to be a huge distraction that I don't need or want in my life.

Gently picking her up, I head down the hall towards the bedrooms. I briefly think about putting her in the room I gave her last night but instead carry her to my room, putting her under the covers before crawling in beside her.

Her unconscious body curls right into me and I wrap my arms around her. If I keep this up, I'm going to get attached and everyone I have ever been attached to dies.

Just like my sweet little sister. Only, she may not be dead now. If she's not, I will have Markayla to thank for that. Without her, I might not have ever known it was a possibility.

I lay there for several hours rubbing Markayla's back as she sleeps on my chest. Eventually, I slip out of the bed and go back to my computer to work through more of the files.

If my sister is still out there that means she is still waiting for me to come rescue her. She knows that I would never give up on her.

The thought that I kind of did give up sends a pain through my chest. Back then it never occurred to me that the morgue could be lying about the identity of the body they said was my sister.

The image of her burning to death has played havoc in my nightmares for the last couple of years.

But now to imagine what she may have been suffering this whole time might just kill me. It could be worse than what I originally thought.

It's time to find out and to make everyone ever involved pay for the hell she has gone through.

"I'm coming, Mel." I say out loud as I continue through the files.

Not all of them have a picture to go with the name or the file so the facial recognition software won't work on all of it. It can, however, help with a huge amount of the ones that do.

There's so many fucking files. So many women. Even if my sister isn't in here, my club will make sure all these women are rescued and these bastards pay with their lives.

"Back at it already?" I hear from behind me.

"Yeah. If my sister is in these files, I want to find her." I say, opening up a new window as I lay a picture of my sister on the scanner.

"What are you doing?" She asks, watching me.

"I can get the software I have on this computer to compare my sister's face to that of the pictures in the files. It'll flag any that are a close resemblance to her." I explain, although I'm not used to having to do so.

The guys in my club typically leave me to do what I do without interference. I thought I liked it that way. For some reason, having to explain as I go to Markayla doesn't bother me all that much.

"You have facial recognition software?" She says in awe. "But not all the files have a picture." She looks back at me.

"True. All of those we will need to go through with a fine tooth comb."

"That's thousands of files." Her eyes widen at the thought.

"Yeah, so get busy. I made you a basic list of characteristics to look for so you can set the ones aside that are similar in comparison." I smile, handing her a piece of paper.

"I still think we need more than just us." She comments, taking a seat next to me with the computer I gave her earlier.

"Well, none of my brothers can help with this right now. You have any suggestions?" I ask almost sarcastically knowing that her adoptive brother is out looking for her.

"Actually, I might." Her chin juts out, staring at me.

"Okay. Who do you suggest?" I ask, turning to her fully. I'm extremely curious as to who she will suggest.

"Alessandro. That's who." She says quickly.

"Who is Alessandro?" I growl as a wave of something I have never felt before runs through me. I know exactly what it is and it pisses me off even more that I feel it. The secretive smile on her face tells me she suspects my feelings.

"My cousin. Everyone else calls him Baratta but I grew up calling him by his first name." She explains although her grin doesn't fade.

"Can you trust him?" I ask.

"I think so." She looks distant for a second before straightening her back. "Yes, we can trust him."

"Then call him. But listen, I'm putting a lot of trust in you here with this. If he does anything to jeopardize this...I'll kill him." I say with as much seriousness as I can. Her eyes widen again but she shakes her head, smiling as she looks back at me.

"I believe that you would try and maybe you would succeed. I promise you, he can be

trusted. He never breaks his word if he gives it."
She says without looking away.

I shake my head again before she stands up, leaving the room to get her phone. Meanwhile, I turn back to my computer.

What the hell did she mean, maybe I would succeed? Just who the hell is this guy? I ask myself.

Markkayla

My hands shake as I turn my phone back on after having it off this whole time. It dings repeatedly with voicemails and text messages.

Without even looking at those, I scroll down to the phone number I have for Alessandro. I'm really not sure how this conversation is going to go.

Quickly hitting the number, I hear it connect as it begins to ring on the other end before I hear him answer in his deep accented voice.

"KayKay, how nice of you to call me back. I've been trying to reach you since yesterday." He drawls out calmly.

"Oh, did you call? I only just turned my phone back on but didn't check any of my messages." I say quickly, trying my best to keep my voice from quivering.

"Hmm." He says by way of a response. "So where exactly are you, my sweet cousin?" He asks quietly.

"I need you to promise me two things before I tell you that. One, you will not tell Papa Tony where I am and two, you will help me find someone." I say, then wait for his response.

"Why would I promise you these things?" He says on a laugh.

"Because you love me and because you swore to me years ago that you would always be there for me, even if it meant going against the family." My chin juts out even though he can't see me.

"I could just promise and not keep it." He says, although I can tell he's smiling which is something I know he rarely does.

"Ah, but you won't. Once you give your word, you always keep it." I laugh knowingly.

"I should have known you would be a thorn in my side. Now, tell me where you are." He says.

"Give me your word first." I stand my ground making sure he swears it.

"Fine. I give you my word. Satisfied?" He asks.

"Nope. Say all of it. I know how you work, Alessandro." I smile into the phone.

"I give you my word that I will not tell Papa Tony and that I will help you to find someone. Even though you have yet to tell me who that someone is." He says on a rushed sigh as if it killed him to say it.

"Great! I just texted you the address." I answer.

"I'll see you in ten minutes." He says quickly.

"Ten minutes?" I ask but he's already hung up the call.

How the fuck is he already so close by? He's supposed to be in South America. I think to myself.

Alessandro Baratta

I knew my cousin Markayla would call me eventually. While we did receive word that she was currently safe, my Uncle sent me to protect her.

He's currently in Colorado setting up a safe house for my Aunt who everyone else believes is dead. According to the sources I contacted in my hunt for her whereabouts, she was supposed to have been killed by the man Joey had hired.

Instead, that man had sold her off in the slave trade down in South America. Luckily, other than being beaten, she had not been harmed in other ways.

Even so, I took great pleasure in dispatching all of those who had harmed her, including Joey's hired man.

I don't remember his name now. I never remember their names. Why should I remember the names of monsters that could do what they do to women and sometimes, children?

I don't have any problems sleeping at night. But then again, the doctors used to say there was something wrong with me. They were right. Even I can admit that I'm not what most people call normal.

When I realized that I was different, I did a lot of research on the subject. Sociopath is what they labeled me. I don't hurt people who don't truly deserve it though.

As for love, I know I love my Aunt and Uncle. Even my sweet Cousin Markayla. She always took up for me, no matter what it was that I had done. I've never felt that protective of anyone else before.

Well, except Fiona. The beautiful, feisty, tattoo artist has gotten under my skin. She doesn't know it yet, but I'll be back for her.

Grabbing my bag off the bed, I leave the small motel room leaving the key on the table. No need to do a check out. They'll figure it out later.

Most people only get these kinds of rooms so they have a place to do their shady business without witnesses. I get them to remain hidden.

Chapter 5
Markayla

My heart has been hammering since Alessandro got here thirty minutes ago. Introducing Buzz to him caused even more nervousness. The way the two of them looked at each other told me that if either moved the wrong way in the slightest, neither would hesitate slitting the other's throat.

I left it mostly up to Buzz to bring him up to speed on what has been going on and what we need help with.

"I've never seen this type of facial recognition software before. Where did you get it?" Alessandro asks.

"I created it." Buzz answers, never looking up from the system.

"Nice. We should still probably tap into the system the FBI has though." Alessandro suggests getting Buzz's full attention.

"You have access to that?" Buzz asks quickly.

"I can get access. Yes." He confirms. "Let me make some calls. I'll need your IP address." He hands Buzz a notepad to write it down before leaving the room.

"Who exactly is your cousin?" Buzz asks, still staring at the door Alessandro walked out of.

"That is his story to tell. All I can say is that he is a good man that keeps his word. Always." I answer the best way that I can without actually telling my cousin's secrets.

Even if I were threatened with death, I would never give up information where he is concerned. I'm one of the very few who even have a way to contact him. No one else actually knows that though. If they did, my life would have been in danger years ago.

"It's all set. You should be getting an email from an unknown address. Click the link, it'll connect you automatically." Alessandro announces, walking back into the room.

"Holy shit." Buzz breathes out a few minutes later as the software starts to take over all the screens.

"Pretty cool. Yes?" Alessandro sits down in a chair, opening a laptop that is connected to the files. "Now, let's see what we can find in these."

"I don't know what kind of connections you've got to be able to get into this system but I want them." Buzz's entire face is lit up as he watches it work.

"I'm afraid I can't give you that." Alessandro holds a small smile on his face.

"Why not?" Buzz asks.

"Because I would have to kill you. While it may be a promise that my sweet cousin did not get from me to not do, I don't think she would appreciate me slitting your throat." He replies so calmly, I have to hold back my giggle.

I know that he is serious in his answers while others usually think he's joking around. My cousin never jokes though.

"Who are you?" Buzz asks seriously. Alessandro doesn't answer though. He just sits there working with that secret little smile he always has. Buzz turns back to his own computer getting back to work.

I look at Buzz's profile, studying him while he's busy. He's so damn handsome, my stomach flops just from looking at him.

I want more of him but I'm not sure exactly how he feels about what happened between us and I of course, would never ask.

It's possible he regrets it happening. He's not tried to kiss me since I woke up in his bed. Actually he's not touched me at all.

I really don't even know this man so I'm not sure why the hell I care so much.

Buzz

We all work in silence as we try to go through the files. My mind wonders for the hundredth time who exactly this Alessandro Baratta is.

I send what I do know plus a picture that my security camera caught to a friend of mine that works in the higher up offices of the military.

My club has worked with him for a while now. He was beneficial in finding the warehouse where the first set of girls were being held prisoner when the Wolfsbane Ridge MC was looking for Officer Wilson's niece a little while back.

I catch Markayla shifting in her seat out of the corner of my eye. I've not been able to get her out of my head either. Neither of us have said anything about what happened between us.

I'm not even sure how to explain what happened between us. She's getting under my skin and I barely know her.

All the women I typically sleep with know the score up front. Don't get attached because I most definitely won't be staying.

I refuse to think about the fact that I placed her in my own bed. I've never allowed a woman to sleep in my own bed. She seems to be a first for me and I'm not exactly sure how I feel about it.

Thinking about the way her body fit so well against my own has my cock stirring behind my zipper. No woman has ever had that ability. Another first that is pissing me off.

"I'm going to step outside for a few minutes." I say quickly, standing up and leaving the room without a backwards glance.

I light up a cigarette as soon as I step outside, pulling it deep into my lungs. Not wanting to think any more about Markayla, I pull my phone out and dial Skeeter.

"Hey, man." Skeeter answers distractedly.

"Hey, something wrong over there?" I ask, immediately alert.

"Not exactly sure yet but a couple of the women that were pulled from the last warehouse are missing from the safe houses we put them in." Skeeter explains.

"Are you sure they didn't just leave on their own?" I ask.

"That's what I'm not sure about yet. We told them all they could leave whenever they wanted to so it is possible a few decided to not stay where they were. Plus they weren't all in the same safe house. So we just don't know yet." He explains further.

"Let me know if you need me." I say.

"Soon as we know more, I'll let you know. So what's up on your end?" He asks.

"Markayla got her cousin here to help us. He apparently has some major connections." I answer, looking back at the door.

"This cousin wouldn't happen to be Alessandro Baratta, would it?" Skeeter asks, surprising me.

"It would." I answer with a smile.

"Does he know you know who he is?" Skeeter asks in a hushed tone.

"But I don't know who he is." I state calmly as Skeeter laughs.

"You just be careful where the Ghost is concerned. I would hate to die trying to kill the real deal to avenge your death." He chuckles through the phone.

"I get the feeling that Markayla is correct where her cousin is concerned. He's a man of his word." I elaborate.

"Timber told me the same when I talked to him last." Skeeter says.

"How is Officer Wilson's daughter doing?" I ask with concern. She was in pretty bad shape when we found her in the warehouse.

"She's on the mend. Refuses to leave Blood's room in the clubhouse." He says.

"I bet that makes Officer Wilson feel good." I laugh, thinking about the serious man I met.

"Yeah, but we would be the same damn way." Skeeter laughs.

"I would probably already have shot Blood in the head and carried her home." I state matter of factly.

"I'm sure you would have." He answers, knowing me so well. "Check back in later. I need to look more into these girls that have disappeared again." He says before hanging up.

I sit outside a few minutes longer before heading back in. Hopefully I can concentrate on the files instead of Markayla's presence.

I'm just grabbing a bottle of water in the kitchen when Alessandro walks in behind me.

"Want to tell me what's going on between you and my cousin?" He asks, grabbing his own water from the fridge.

"I don't know what you mean." I answer.

"I saw how you were watching her from the corner of your eye and I saw how she watches you when she thinks you are not looking." He says with a little smile.

"There's nothing going on between Markayla and I, Alessandro." I answer quickly but even I know that to be a lie.

"Well, let me just say, if there was something going on and you hurt her in any way, I will slit your throat and dump your corpse somewhere no one will ever find it. And, call me Baratta please. Only Markayla gets away with the Alessandro business." He says with a smile, slapping me on the back as he walks out.

Markayla

I hear Buzz come back from outside, going into the kitchen. My cousin went in that direction right after and I hope they are both getting along. I can hear them talking in there although I can't make out what they are saying.

The next file that I pull up catches my eye. The file is labeled as a buyer and it's the name that catches me. Peter Cassio. The description sounds exactly like Pecker Pete.

I never had much to do with the men that came to the house to see Joey. They all gave me extremely bad vibes.

"Hey, guys?" I say as Buzz and Alessandro walk back into the room.

"Find something?" Buzz walks over quickly.

"I think I found Pecker Pete. There's no picture but there's other information here. Looks like sales receipts, each marked with different numbers." I say, turning the laptop to the two of them so that they can see.

"Those are locations." Alessandro murmurs.

"Locations?" I ask.

"GPS coordinates." Buzz answers, looking over at Alessandro.

"Send that file to my phone." Alessandro says, turning for the door.

"Where are you going?" I ask quickly.

"To check the locations in the file that are close by." He answers as if talking to a simpleton.

"I'm coming with you." Buzz stands up in a hurry.

"What about me?" I ask with concern.

"Both of you should stay here. Continue going through the files. Look for more files with Pecker Pete's name on it. I doubt there's anything still at the locations listed. I just need to check them out for clues." Alessandro answers.

"Well it should be safe enough then right? I can come too." I argue.

"No." Both men growl at the same time.

"He's right although I don't like it. It's unlikely there's anything left at these locations." Buzz says, looking at me. "But you'll call if that changes right? I don't want to miss an opportunity to find my sister." He says directly to Alessandro.

"I give you my word, I will call if there's something there." Alessandro answers before walking out the door.

Chapter 6
Markayla

It's been three days since my cousin left to check the various locations in the file. The few that were here in New Orleans didn't have anything. He said it was as if they cleaned the entire place. But eventually there will be something someone missed somewhere. I think he's now in Florida checking out a place that is actually off the grid in the Everglades.

Buzz has practically avoided me since Alessandro left. There haven't been any more invites to watch a movie on the couch. Even eating together is a no go. He always takes his food to eat while he works.

I help as much as I can, continuing to slowly go through the files one by one. It's becoming a tedious boring task as I so rarely find one that sounds similar to his sister.

I'm just getting out of the shower, wrapping my towel around my body as I open the door to head to my room across the hall on the third night when I almost walk straight into him in the hallway.

"I'm sorry. I didn't hear you coming down the hall." I breathe out quickly as my heart rate jumps up. I'm fully aware that all I have around me is a towel as his electric eyes hold my own.

He doesn't say a word as he reaches up with his hand, skimming his fingertips along the tops of my breasts just above my towel.

"Always so beautiful and so fucking distracting." He murmurs, never losing eye contact.

I feel my core immediately slicken with anticipation from his slight touch. Licking my dry lips, I watch as his eyes follow the movement.

So I affect him just as much as he affects me. I think to myself. But then, he drops his hand, moving towards his bedroom and shuts the door without a backwards glance.

Just that little bit of touching from him has me completely worked up. I still don't know him all that well but from what I have seen since I've been here, I like a lot. It's not just his looks that attract me.

The way he works tirelessly looking for his sister even though we are not yet sure that it is her. The way he always makes sure that I have everything that I need. He's a true gentleman that happens to wear leather.

Making my way into my own room, I gently close the door. A few minutes later, I'm under the covers falling asleep into dreams of a man that calls to me with just his eyes.

Buzz

It takes me a while to fall asleep after leaving Markayla standing in the hall. It felt like the hardest thing I have ever done in my life.

I could tell from the way her eyes looked at me that it wouldn't take much to have her against the wall while I sunk myself deep within her.

I'm still not sure exactly what is going on with me where she is concerned. I've watched her every day since being here.

Even though she really doesn't have to, she works just as long as I do on the files looking for clues about Melody.

I'm afraid that I'm becoming attached to her and that can be a bad thing. In the line of work that my club is in, it can be very dangerous. For ourselves and anyone who is involved with us.

Several of the brothers have families and I'm not too sure how they handle telling them goodbye each day knowing it could be the last time they see them.

The feelings that I'm currently experiencing where Markayla is concerned have me thinking that I would like to see where it goes. Maybe she would be up for that after this whole thing is over.

I finally fall asleep dreaming about the hell my sister may be going through. In my dream the face of Mel changes into the face of Markayla. I wake in a pool of sweat.

Instead of trying to sleep a bit more, I head straight into my computer room, getting right back to work.

That's where Markayla finds me when she finally wakes around seven a.m.

"Find anything yet?' She asks.

"Not yet." I answer as my phone begins to ring.

Looking at it, I see that it's a call from Skeeter.

"I need to step outside for a minute." I tell her, walking quickly towards the door.

"We got a tip." Skeeter says as soon as the call connects.

"What is it?" I say with anticipation.

"We've had guys stationed at all the local clubs that Joey and his associates are known to frequent. Joey was seen at the Blue Black last night with a guy named Peter. The stupid shits talked openly even with so many people around." Skeeter relays the information.

"How do we know for sure the guy's name is Peter?" I ask with my heart hammering in my chest.

"Ranger was able to sit close enough to listen in on their conversation.' He says.

Ranger wouldn't make a mistake on the names if he was the one there. It's just as important to him as it is to me to find Melody.

"They are supposed to be back there tonight. They kept talking about a woman they needed to get rid of. Ranger wasn't sure of who the woman was. We suspect it to be Markayla, they said they needed to find her first." He says quickly.

"Baratta is gone looking at other locations. I'll go to the Blue Black tonight. Maybe we can catch this Peter guy. I suspect he's the one that has my sister. At least we think he does." I answer.

"For yours and Ranger's sake, I really do hope it is Melody." Skeeter says.

"So do I."

"Look, I'll send Ranger and a few others to meet you there. Please try to bring them in alive, Buzz." He growls the last part because he knows me so well.

I tend to black out in my rage. By the time I come back to myself, the fuckers that pissed me off are dead and I'm left to feed them to the alligators in the Bayou.

"No worries, I need them alive too. My sister's life may depend on it." I answer back before we disconnect the call.

Walking back inside, I find Markayla bent over in the kitchen looking for a pan. I can't stop myself from standing there and admiring her ass.

It's just the right thickness that tapers down into shapely legs that I'm once again thinking about wrapping around me.

Unable to stop myself, I walk until my front is pressed against her back side causing her to stand up from her position. My cock is already hard as hell behind my zipper.

"I'll be out for a few hours this evening." I breathe into her ear, running my nose along the shell.

Her breathing immediately kicks up a notch. She's so damn responsive to my touch. I fucking love it!

I keep standing there, pressed against her, waiting for just a small sign that she is more than willing. It doesn't take long, she pushes her ass harder back into me.

Wrapping my arms around her, my hands push up her shirt exposing her braless nipples to my hungry fingers.

"I want you, Markayla." I whisper again.

"I want you too." She answers.

"How much? Shall we see?" I ask, skimming my hands down to her pants which I push down to her thighs quickly.

Bringing my right hand back up, I run it along her slit and find her absolutely soaking wet for me.

"Fuck! You don't know what you do to me." I admit.

My left hand comes up to her breasts, flicking her nipple until she moans.

"Please, Reese." She moans.

The way she says my name in that breathy way has me ready to bend her over right here and plunge into her as deep as I can in the middle of the kitchen.

I wonder if it would frighten her to know that I'm not exactly gentle. I like it rough.

"What if I bend you over right here? Plunge deep inside of you from behind? What if I don't want to be gentle?" I ask her seriously.

"Yes, please." She breathes out just as my right hand feels her desire gush from her core.

"Fuck, you're perfect." I growl, making quick work of my jeans.

I barely get them down to my thighs before I rock my hardness along her hot center, coating myself in her juices. I'm lining myself up to slam in right at the time I remember a condom. Pulling back, I find one quickly in my pocket, getting it on in record time.

I give no indication for her to be ready for me after that, as I bend her forward with my hand on her back and slamming my hardness deep inside.

Her core tightens up around me in a tight grip. I try to give her a minute to get used to me but I can't hold back. Pulling nearly all the way out, I slam back inside as hard as I can. My balls slapping her flesh.

"Harder." she moans out and I am happy to oblige.

It doesn't take long until she's screaming out her pleasure while pushing me into my own.

Fuck, this woman is perfect. I think a few minutes later. *I'm so fucking screwed.*

Markayla

After our sex marathon in the kitchen, we both went back to working on the files. So far we have around ten that match a good description of Melody but none mention Pecker Pete.

"Where are you going?" I ask, watching him put things into a backpack to take with him as well as a few guns.

"To the Blue Black. Joey was spotted there yesterday." He says but it seems like he's not telling me everything.

"When will you be back?"

"Maybe just a few hours. Here's the code to disable the system to get out of the warehouse and back in just in case you need to get out of here quickly." He explains.

"No one has found us here yet, I'll be fine." I say with conviction.

"Yeah, everything will be fine. I'll be back in a few hours." He grabs his bag swinging it up onto his shoulder.

He turns towards the door taking a few steps before he turns back towards me. He grabs me quickly, kissing me deeply before releasing me. I'm still standing there in shock when I hear the door close behind him.

Four hours later, I'm still alone and starving. There's literally nothing in the fridge. We've mostly survived on take out since I've been here. Even all the breakfast makings are gone.

Looking over at the code to the door, I think about running down to the closest store to pick up a few things. Surely, I could get there and back before anyone realizes anything.

Making my decision, I grab my purse after putting on my shoes and head out the door. I left my cell by the computers because I don't want to be tracked by it.

Joey probably has someone watching for my phone to come back on the grid. It's best if it's not with me.

I make it out to the road, looking all around me, I don't see anything out of place. Turning left, I walk quickly towards the store I remember seeing on our way here.

Too bad I didn't pay closer attention to the van parked at the end of the street. It would have possibly saved me from the hell that was coming my way.

Buzz

"Well that was a fucking waste of time." I growl, looking around the room at my brothers in the clubhouse.

"I can't believe they didn't show up. Did they get tipped off that we would be there?" Ranger stomps around the room, trying to contain his own anger.

"Either someone tipped them off or it was all a setup from the beginning." Mick, our road captain says from his chair.

"What do you mean?" I ask, seriously.

"Doesn't anyone in this room find it rather convenient that they would talk about this shit so free out in the open?" He looks each man in the eyes around the table.

"He does have a point." Skeeter, runs his hand over his face.

"These guys haven't gotten this far by being that stupid." Grim comments from across the room.

"If it was a setup, then why didn't they attack while we were there?" Tanker asks.

We all sit quietly thinking for a few minutes before Ranger speaks up again.

"A diversion for something. They needed us out of the way?" He forms it into a question and my mind automatically pulls up Markayla's face.

"Fuck!" I yell, pulling my phone from my pocket to dial her number but it just rings without an answer.

"I left Markayla at the warehouse alone. She's not answering her phone. Fuck!" I explain, dialing her number yet again.

"Go back to your warehouse and check everything out. Mick? Ranger? You two go with him. The rest of you, get out there and see if you can find these assholes again." Skeeter demands from the head of the table.

I waste no time getting out the door to my bike. Revving the engine, I take off down the road without waiting for the other guys. I know they'll be right behind me.

Chapter 7
Markayla

I slowly begin to wake up, my eyes feeling so heavy I have to concentrate to get them to open all the way.

At first, I'm confused about where I'm at but then everything that happened comes rushing back.

I was headed down to the store when someone grabbed me from behind, placing a cloth over my mouth and nose. My last thought before blackness took me was that I would probably never wake up again.

As my eyes open to the room around me, I can see that it almost looks like a normal bedroom. One you would expect to see at an unsavory motel. At least it's not a basement with a metal table.

I'm just sitting up on the bed, looking around and noticing there's no windows when I hear the door being unlocked.

Looking in that direction, I'm unsurprised to see Joey step through it with his slimy smile.

"About time you woke up. Are you hungry?" He asks, reaching back outside the door to someone I can't see that hands him a tray of food.

I continue to sit there, not saying a word even though he continues to talk happily like I'm not being held prisoner here.

"I'll be back later this evening and we can have a nice quiet dinner together. That sound good?" His smile slips for only a second as I continue my silence.

"I will see you later my sweet, Markayla and we can discuss your new role as my fiancée." He smirks when I flinch at his words.

The door slams shut behind him and I hear the lock engage yet again.

Fuck! What am I going to do? I know him. He'll take me tonight, by force if he has to. No one will know where I'm at. Do I even have anyone that would even look for me? I think to myself.

Buzz's face flashes into my head. I would have loved to see where we could have gone in our relationship. I'm not even certain what we had could be called a relationship.

Unable to hold back the tears, I lay down crying silently into the pillow.

Buzz

"Why the fuck would you leave her completely alone?" Baratta growls from across the table.

It's the most emotion I've seen him display since we first met.

"It's not like I thought she would leave on her own. I only gave her the code to get out in case of emergencies." I growl back, tired of his shit.

"That's enough out of both of you. Screaming at each other isn't going to help a fucking thing right now." Skeeter says, trying to calm the tension in the room.

"I want to know how the fuck they even knew she was there!" I say through clenched teeth.

"I'm starting to think we have a traitor in our club." Mick calmly says to the few of us that are in the room. Every brother there goes as still as a statue.

"You think it could be one of us?" Ranger comments from against the wall.

"If you'll notice, I didn't call in everyone for this meeting. I think all of you in this room are completely loyal. As for the rest, I'm not entirely sure about." Skeeter sighs.

"Some of the guys not here have been with the club for years." Tanker leans his hands on the table, looking at Skeeter.

"Yeah, they have but someone, for some reason, has gone over to the other side. The last few weeks several of the girls that were saved from the warehouse in Belle Chaise have come up missing from the safe houses we stashed them in. Only the brothers in this club knew where those safe houses were!" Mick says to the room.

"So what are we going to do about it?" Ranger asks.

It's odd for a prospect to be in on these meetings. I suspect Skeeter asked him to be here because he and I have been friends for an extremely long time. We are all hopeful that the path we are on will lead us to my sister.

My mind wanders to Markayla. I get an ache in my chest at the thought of her being harmed in any way. Over the days that we have spent together, she has somehow gotten under my skin. I'm not entirely sure if I will ever be able to get her out.

The guys switch to talk about how to get inside the fortress of a house that Joey is holed up in with his men over in Texas.

That's right, we know exactly where they are. Mainly because I had the foresight to slip a tracking device inside the sole of Markayla's shoes the very first night she was in my apartment.

The same night that I just stood there watching as she slept before going back to my

—

own room only to dream about sinking my hardness into her wet slit with her legs wrapped around me.

"We should get there later tonight. Buzz, we need to make sure that you get their surveillance cameras knocked out. At least for a few minutes. Give all the guys time to take out the guards around the perimeter. Then I want everyone to get inside as fast as possible. Save any women you find along the way." Skeeter explains.

"I'll make sure the guys outside know the plan only at the last minute. I'm also going to make sure they turn over all their cell phones to be locked in the safe until we get back." Mick announces.

"Hopefully that buys us enough time to take these fucks by surprise." Skeeter says.

"Sounds good but I want everyone to know that Joey should be left for me to deal with. He's family and whatever happens to him should be a family decision." Baratta finally speaks up.

"Agreed. Mick will make sure everyone knows to keep that fucker alive." He says, looking to Mick who nods his head once.

"Good, now let's get packed up and ready to head out." Skeeter dismisses us as the meeting is over.

I hang back, wanting to speak with him privately for a minute.

"Something on your mind, Buzz?" Skeeter asks once everyone else has left.

"If he's hurt Markayla in any way, I make no promises about him making it out alive." I murmur looking towards the door.

"Is it like that?" Skeeter asks seriously.

"Like what?" I growl, still not looking directly at him.

"Fine. Play dumb. Or hell, maybe you just don't recognize it yet." He shrugs his shoulders.

"Recognize what?" I finally look over at him, perplexed as to what he could mean.

"That you are gone for that girl." He laughs. "I always wondered if you even had it in you to fall in love. I can't wait to get to know her." He laughs again, slapping me on the back.

"I'm not talking about love." I curl my lip at the thought but Skeeter continues laughing.

"I can't wait until you realize how blind you have been." He says as a parting shot, walking out the door. I can still hear him chuckling as he walks down the hall.

I can't be in love. Hell, we barely know each other. I think to myself although my head whispers slightly that I can't be exactly sure of that.

I think of her beautiful face again and feel an ache in my chest. Fuck! He may be right. Double fuck!

Needing to grab my equipment so that I can work remotely from the van I will be riding in, I head out the door a few minutes later.

I'll think about everything else later. Right now, we just have to make sure we get to Markayla before anything seriously fucked up happens to her.

Markayla

My face is stinging from the slap across my jaw that Joey delivered himself when I attempted to rush the door as soon as it was opened.

He's chatting happily yet again while others bring in a table, setting it up with a shit ton of food as if we are having a huge dinner party.

"Since you can't get up, I'll fix your plate for you, my dear." He smiles graciously in my direction.

This mother fucker is more fucked in the head than I ever imagined before. After knocking me down with the slap to the face, he had his goons tie me to this chair only leaving one hand free. So that I could still eat, he said. If he gets close enough, maybe I can still claw out at least one of his eyes.

The thought makes me smirk.

"See, I knew you could still smile for me. You are way too beautiful to frown so much. What would your mother think?" He says it so softly but my skin crawls with the way he says it as if he knows something that I don't.

"Don't you dare bring my mother into this you bastard." I say through clenched teeth.

His smile never wavers which pisses me off even more.

"Why do you want me anyway?" I finally ask, unable to stay silent any more.

"Have you really not figured it out yet, my sweet?" He laughs.

"Figured out what? Just fucking give a straight answer!" I scream, throwing the plate of food he set down in front of me.

He looks ready to hit me again but goes back to smiling as he makes another plate, setting it in front of me again.

"Throw that one and you will eat it from the floor." He says quietly, having noticed I was reaching for it again.

Instead, I pick up my fork, pushing the food around on the plate. My stomach rumbles loudly reminding me that I never ate the food brought to me earlier in the day.

Taking a smile bite of the potatoes, I try to see if I notice anything odd about the taste. Not tasting anything, I continue eating, waiting for Joey to elaborate.

"With you by my side, I can own everything that should have been mine long ago." He takes a bite of his steak.

"What should have been yours?" I ask.

"Everything. Every part of the family business should have been mine. Instead your Papa Tony betrayed my father, placing himself in line to be head of the family. If I make you mine, then I get to have it all. Including your fathers personal investments. Once he's dead of course." His comments confuse me at first.

"My father?" I ask, unsure of his meaning.

"Tony Marcus." He says as if talking to a child.

"But Papa Tony isn't my real father." I say, he begins to laugh.

"Poor stupid little Markayla. They told that lie hoping it would keep you safe. They backed it up by Tony not showing any emotions when it came to you. You are a true Marcus. And you will be even more of a Marcus once I make you my wife." His statement has me reeling trying to keep up.

Even if Tony Marcus were my real father wouldn't that mean that Joey is my cousin? And he wants to make me his wife? Eww!

"That would mean you are my real cousin, Joey! That makes it even more gross!" I throw down my fork.

Looking down I realize that I have finished everything on my plate. I'm also feeling extremely tired. My eyes do not want to stay open.

Looking back at Joey, he's back to grinning again.

"I will have your body tonight. I've waited long enough." He whispers to me, licking his lips.

I'm unable to respond. I've lost the ability to do so. The last thing I see before darkness takes me yet again is the excitement on Joey's face.

Buzz

"Everyone in position?" I ask quietly over the coms in my ear.

I listen as everyone checks in, confirming that they are in fact where they are supposed to be.

"Turning off cameras in three…two…one. GO!" I say through the mic.

There's total silence in the night, just as Skeeter wanted it to be. We didn't want them alerted to anything going on around the perimeter until we breached the door.

Things never go as planned though. Even in the military you learn that shit. Gun fire sounds from the East side of the perimeter. Then all hell breaks loose.

Jumping from the van, I grab my gun, running towards the front door. I catch a glimpse of Baratta, who seems to be taking his time getting to the door.

Without even looking up, he points his gun to a guy on the second floor, pulling the trigger. I watch as his body falls over the railing and landing with a thud on the ground.

He sees me looking in his direction. He smiles back, shrugging his shoulders before walking on towards the front door.

Both of us go in at the same time. Him taking out the guys to the right as I take out the ones coming from the hall on the left.

"Let me know if you find Markayla or Tony." He says quietly, moving off. I nod back in reply, walking quickly but quietly down the hall.

I meet several jackasses coming from another door that I take out quickly. They definitely were not counting on us breaching the inside.

That's when I see him. Joey Marcus walks out of a room appearing half dressed, surrounded by his bodyguards.

Catching sight of me, they fire in my direction and I duck down behind a wall, returning fire. I know I hit at least one of them as they yell out.

Finally the bullets stop and I peek around the wall. Looking down the hall. There's two dead men lying in their own blood.

Joey and the others must have made a run for it through the door behind them.

"Baratta, spotted Joey. He left through a door at the end of the hall. I think it's a stairwell." I say through the coms.

"I've got it. Find Markayla." He says quickly. I could hear gunfire on his end. I smile, hoping it's Joey he's shooting at.

Getting to the door they came out of, I slowly open it, looking inside. It's completely dark but I can see that it's a bedroom with a bed that looks occupied.

Turning on the lights, I can see that it is Markayla. She's completely naked, stretched out on the bed like some sort of sacrifice.

My stomach burns that I may not have gotten to her in time. Rushing forward, I check her pulse and see that she is breathing fine. She doesn't wake up though which scares me even more. The only thing I can see wrong with her on the outside is a bruise on her cheek.

I need to get her out of here and to a doctor as soon as possible. There's no telling what that fucker gave to her or did to her while she was unconscious.

Chapter 8
Buzz

We are all sitting here waiting for word on Markayla's condition in the hospital waiting room when Baratta finally arrives.

"Any word?" He asks, walking up to me.

"Not yet. They wouldn't let me back there because I'm not family." I growl out, still pissed off that Skeeter stopped me from throttling nurse ratchet when she refused me entry.

"Her father will be up here in a minute. He'll get some answers." Baratta says just as the doors open revealing a man in an expensive suit with graying hair.

"I'm Markayla Marcus' father. Can you please take me to her room please. I would also like to see her doctor." He speaks with authority.

At first, I think the nurse is going to refuse but after checking her charts that show him as an emergency contact, she stands up to lead the way.

Looking behind him, he sees me standing there and gives me a nod.

"That means you should follow." Baratta says to me quietly.

Not asking how he even knows that, I fall in next to Mr. Marcus as we are led down the hall towards the rooms.

"Thank you, young man." Marcus looks over at me.

"You're welcome." I answer automatically.

"Do you have feelings for her?" He asks out of nowhere.

"What?" I ask, looking over at him quickly.

"My daughter. Do you have feelings for her?" He asks again, not looking away.

I'm left speechless, unsure of how to answer that question. It's something I've tried not to think much about over the last several days.

"Hmm. So you haven't decided yet. When you figure it out, we can talk again." He says just before we walk into her room.

She looks so small lying on that bed, still unconscious.

"Shouldn't she be awake already?" I ask out loud.

"Not with the amount of sleeping pills she was given." A doctor says, walking into the room. "Mr. Marcus, I'm Doctor Simmons. Your daughter appears to be just fine other than some bruising on her face. At this time we are just letting the sleeping pills wear off. We are making sure she stays hydrated with the IV we put into her arm. It should help push it all from her system more quickly." He explains, looking through his chart.

"She wasn't..." I gulp, trying again. "She wasn't touched in any other way?" I ask.

"Not as far as we can tell. We went ahead with a rape kit just in case but we didn't find any indications that it was needed." His report eases the ache in my chest a little bit.

I stay only a few minutes more to ensure that she is alright before I say a quiet goodbye and letting Tony Marcus know that I will check back in on her later.

I have to get back to trying to find the guy that possibly has my sister. I'm trying to think if there was something I missed in the one file we found on the stupid fucker as I walk back into the waiting room.

"How is she?" Skeeter asks, standing up from his seat.

"The doctor says she should recover without any lasting effects." I say to the men standing around.

"We got there in time?" Baratta asks quietly from beside me.

"It looks like it." I reply.

"Good. Let's go." He strides towards the door not waiting to see if I follow.

"Where are we going?" I ask, trying to keep up.

"To have a nice little chat with Joey of course." He smiles over at me. It's not a nice smile so I highly doubt the little chat will be pleasant. At least, not for Joey.

The thought makes my body start to hum just as it always does before I hurt someone who deserves it.

"Just a few rules before we get there. You can't do anything that will kill him. What happens to him in that regard is family business." He comments a few minutes later when we are on the road.

"I'll try to hold back." I growl through my teeth.

"I know you want justice for Markayla and your sister too, just as much as the rest of us. There will be justice there but it will be dished out by family. It's the way it is with us. Yes?" He explains and I think I finally get it.

It's the same way when you are in the MC. You are a brother, family and if you betray the family then the family deals with you.

"Not a problem. But at least tell me I can make him bleed." I roll my eyes at the thought of not doing so.

Baratta just laughs at my question.

"We will definitely make him bleed. We need to find your sister. Yes?" He smiles in my direction.

"Yes." I answer simply, my heart speeding up at the thought of finding her.

Markayla

I wake up surrounded by white walls and wonder if I'm dead already. As I wipe my hair from my face a sharp pain makes me wince.

"Nope. Not dead." I whisper into the silence but jump when I hear a voice speak back to me.

"Not dead my sweet girl." Papa Tony is sitting in a chair across the room from me.

He smiles in my direction but I'm not sure how I should react. Should I scream until someone comes in here? I think to myself as I glance towards the door.

"Hmm. Why are you so afraid of me?" He asks as if he honestly doesn't know.

"Where's Joey?" I ignore his question, asking one of my own. My heart pounds with thoughts of Joey walking in the door at any second.

"Your cousin has him tied up at the moment." He comments like tying people up is an everyday thing.

Come to think of it, in our family it probably is. If anyone were to hear our conversation they would most likely think he meant they were at the office in the middle of some business.

They would have no clue as to how true that assessment actually is for my cousin Alessandro. While I have never been afraid of him hurting me, I know exactly what kind of man he is. No one would want him as an enemy.

"I think we have a few things to discuss, mia figlia." He says, calling me daughter in Italian.

"I'm not your daughter." I simply say but he stands up slowly walking towards me anyway with a heavy sigh.

"Maybe after you talk to someone that is truly important to us both, you will feel differently." He pulls his phone from his pocket, pushing a few buttons before holding it to his ear.

"It's time, mio caro." He says softly into the phone. That's what he always called my mother. My dear, in Italian.

Holding the phone out to me, I take it from his hand, looking at the unknown number on the screen.

"I will give you some privacy while I go find us some dinner. I'll send out for one of those milk shakes you love so much." He smiles, leaving through the door.

How the hell does he know about the milk shakes?

Shaking my head, I slowly lift the phone to my ear.

"Hello?" I ask.

The voice that answers back has me tearing up instantly.

"Mia Figlia." The sweetest voice in the world says to me.

"Momma? Oh my God! Momma!" I break down while she whispers sweetly to me over the phone trying to explain everything at once.

Apparently, my cousin found evidence a little more than a year ago that my mother was still alive.

Once he found a trail that he could follow, Papa Tony met up with him to try to find my mother. At the time, they didn't know that Joey was behind the whole thing.

By the time they had figured it out, Joey had already taken over nearly every aspect of my life. To keep me safe, they did not try to contact me or let me in on what was going on.

Alessandro and Papa Tony found my mother working as a slave down in South America somewhere. She was being beaten nearly every day but other than that, she didn't suffer from being raped. I guess I can thank God for that little piece of mind.

She goes on to explain about them keeping it hidden that Papa Tony is my real father. While I don't agree that it was the best decision, I can understand their motive behind it.

As we get off the phone, she tells me that Papa Tony will bring me to where she is staying after they release me from the hospital.

My heart swells at the thought of her hugging me again. The last year and a half of my life have been the hardest to endure.

You never realize just how important your parents are in your life until you lose one. Especially the one you are closest to.

My mother was always there for me and I can't put into words just how happy I am to find out that she's still in this world with me.

"Feel better?" I hear Papa Tony from the door. I can't stop the smile on my face as I look back at him.

"Yes. Definitely." I answer.

"I found the Doctor on my way down to get us some food. He says you can probably leave here later today." He places a tray down in front of me as well as my favorite milkshake.

"How did you know about the milkshake?" I help but ask, truly confused.

"I know way more than you think, my daughter. From today onward, we will get to know each other again." He smiles, taking a huge bite from his hamburger.

I smile back as I drink my milkshake, happier today than I've been in a long time.

"Now, about this boy." Papa Tony starts and I almost snort milkshake up my nose at him calling Buzz a boy.

Buzz's face pops into my head before I shake it away. If he cared even a little about me, wouldn't he be here?

"There is no one. I'm just ready to go see mamma." I reply, hoping he won't broach the subject again.

Buzz

Leaving Baratta several hours ago, I swing by my place to get a shower to wash off all the blood that got on me from our little chat with Joey.

He held out a lot longer than I thought he would. I guess being a crazy shit bag can make you endure a lot more pain than a normal man would.

Skeeter has called church for later this afternoon to put together a team that will go with me to Guatemala where Peter Cassio is from.

From the aerial photos I was able to pull up on my computer while I relayed all the information to Skeeter, it looks to be a sprawling mansion on a hillside overlooking the city.

Grabbing my bag, I head out a little earlier hoping to check in on Markayla at the hospital. She should be awake by now.

But what I find when I get there just pisses me right the fuck off.

Storming out of the hospital doors, I dial Baratta's number which he answers on the first ring.

"Where the fuck is she?" I growl through the phone.

"Who?" He asks calmly.

"Your cousin, mother fucker! Where's Markayla!" I demand, seething in anger.

He however has the audacity to laugh through the phone.

"She's with her parents. Besides, what business is it of yours? Hmm? You're not in love with her, right?" I can hear the bastards smile in his voice. I have visions of cutting his tongue out.

"Look, Buzz, you need to concentrate on your sister at the moment. Go save her before it's really too late. In the meantime, give Markayla this time with her parents. After you save your sister, then you can really think about whether or not you are in love with Markayla. Once you know, you can contact me again and I will help you. Yes?" His voice, still so calm is annoying as fuck but I have to admit he's got a point.

"Fine!" I finally say after clenching my teeth so hard I'm sure I've broken more than a few. "But I'm going to hold you to that. Otherwise, I will hunt you down and skin you alive." I growl.

"I wouldn't expect anything less." He says happily before hanging up the phone.

"Fuck!" I mumble once again looking at the phone in my hand. It has a new crack across the screen from my tight grip.

Sticking it back into my pocket, I climb on my bike, laying on the throttle as I head back to the clubhouse.

Chapter 9
Buzz

The day we rescued Markayla, it was almost too easy getting in and wiping out Joey's guys. Most of the men that were loyal to Tony had already left pretty early on when Joey took over leaving only the scum behind.

They were basically easy to pick off one by one. These guys that we are sure to come up against in Guatemala however, will probably give us a fight to remember. I'm looking forward to it!

It's been a little more than a week since I found Markayla gone from the hospital and while I have her phone number, I've yet to call her.

She's not called me either, she probably hasn't thought anything about me since she left. Just thinking about her puts that ache back into my chest like a heavy weight is sitting on top of me.

The boys and I finally got into Guatemala a few hours ago. Luckily, we still have a few contacts down this way that have been keeping tabs on the goings and comings from the house that Pecker Pete owns.

They've managed to get a few pictures of the people around the place. Although they are all kind of blurry from being taken from far away, there is one girl that could possibly be Melody.

The picture is saved to my phone and I've stared at it a lot the last few days. I just hope it's not wishful thinking. Either way, the girls that are there will be saved. That has to count for something.

The guys and I are holed up in a tiny motel that is infested with roaches.

"Have these people never heard of Terminex?" Ranger complains as he stomps yet another bug with a look of disgust.

"Stop being a pussy!" Grim laughs from across the room before jumping away from the wall he was leaning on.

"Alright you fucks. We want to go in about an hour before they find out anyone new has shown up in town. The element of surprise is definitely something we need to use to our advantage. If one of you fuckers accidentally shoots a female, I'm gonna put a cap in your ass myself!" I say to the group around me.

Skeeter wanted Mick to come along with us but none of us wanted to leave him in New Orleans without someone we knew he could trust. So it's just me, Tanker, Grim and Ranger on this mission.

Hopefully we succeed and don't have to send each other back home in a body bag.

"Since there's only one way in and one way out, we should park on this side road here that's a mile out then walk the rest of the way in." Tanker points on the map in front of us.

"Everyone should stay kinda close. They may have a few things rigged around the place." Ranger looks over the wooded area that surrounds the mansion.

"He's right. We hear they have bombs. Need to watch our steps." Gando, one of our Guatemalan contacts says in broken English to the group.

Gando was able to put together a few of his own men to help us out on this mission. He relays all the important information to them because they themselves do not speak English at all.

"Okay. Everyone, be ready to go in thirty." Grim announces.

"Gando. Thanks for doing this man. We will owe you a solid." I say to him.

"You would help if it were my sister." He answers with a smile before I walk away.

Going outside, I light up a smoke, taking a long drag. Just a few more hours and I will know for sure if Melody is still with me or not.

I've missed her sassy comments and smart mouth attitude. Speaking of, there's another woman I've been missing the hell out of but for different reasons.

Pulling out my phone, I stare at it for several long minutes before I pull up her number. But my finger just hovers over the call button.

Maybe I should just send a text. A text is easier isn't it? I don't have to worry about saying the wrong thing.

Me: How are you doing?

I don't expect to get a fast reply but she answers back almost immediately.

Markayla: I'm okay. Just had dinner with my parents.

What else am I supposed to say? I think to myself.

Me: I'm glad you reconnected with your mom.

Markayla: It's been great. Hey, thanks for being there to save me. I don't know what he would have done if you hadn't been there.

Me: Anytime

Markayla: Do you mean that?

Me: Absolutely.

Markayla: I'll hold you to that ;)

I stare at her last message which kind of baffles me. What the hell could she mean by that? Besides, I'm the one that needs to be saved currently. From the ever present hard on I sport every time I even think of her name.

Markayla

I set my phone back on the bedside table with a smile. While I've been on cloud nine with having my mom back in my life, I've been sad since I've been here.

I miss him for some stupid ass reason. What do we really know about each other anyway? The sex is amazing though. Holy hell, the sex is off the charts. But is that a strong enough foundation to work towards something bigger?

"You look lost in thought." My mom says from the door to my room. "That look have anything to do with the young man Alessandro told me about?" She asks with a smile.

"Sort of." I shrug my shoulders. "How did you know Papa Tony was the one for you?" I ask with curiosity.

"I didn't know for sure. We had a whirlwind couple of days together that ended way too soon. I didn't even know who he really was until several months later when he came looking for me." She looks wistful in her thoughts before turning slightly pink. "Those few days were almost completely physical. You know what I am talking about, mia figlia?" She looks at me until I start to turn pink.

I seriously do not want to think about my parents having sex. That is just wrong on so many levels. Instead I shake my head quickly, hoping she'll move on with the story.

"He came back though swearing that he was completely in love. He seemed pissed off about it." She laughs.

"Why would he be pissed about it?" I ask, clearly confused why loving someone would piss you off.

"Because of the lifestyle that he was brought up in. Being a part of the Marcus family is dangerous business. You know this without me needing to tell you." She looks at me with seriousness.

What she is saying is true. It's extremely dangerous.

"Before me and of course you, he only had to worry about himself mostly. With us, he had to worry about keeping us safe as well. I imagine the same holds true for this boy." As she calls him a boy, I giggle remembering Papa Tony calling him that as well.

"I don't think he's in love with me. He did finally message me a few minutes ago to check on me though." I say with a sigh.

"My girl, Alessandro has said that he has that look about him. You mark my words. He'll be back for you. I understand he's currently busy trying to find his sister, but he'll be here. Most likely just as pissed off as your father was." She hugs me close for a few minutes before leaving the room.

As I get ready for bed, I say a silent prayer that Buzz finds his sister and that he stays safe.

Buzz

We walk as silently as possible through the trees leading up to the property, making sure that we take our time with every step carefully so as not to trigger any traps.

We've found quite a few landmines along the way that Tanker has disassembled so that we may get back through this way if need be.

However, I'm hopeful that we kill every one of the fuckers inside that house.

"Wait." The silent whisper comes across our coms.

"What is it, Grim?" I ask just as silently.

"Three goons, ten o'clock." He whispers back.

"We got them." Gando says before he and his men move silently towards the guards.

We never hear a thing as they take them out, slowly laying them down on the ground so even their bodies make no noises.

"There's the fence. Ranger, you're up!" I whisper to him.

He begins to use the cutters to slowly make a hole in the fence. We were surprised to find out that the fence wasn't charged although we were prepared for that scenario as well.

As we all make our way inside the fence, we are caught off guard when a siren starts to blare.

"Well, fuck! I guess they have motion sensors." Tanker says.

"You think?" Grim replies sarcastically.

"Everyone move! Mission is still the same. Take out every one of those fucks, save whoever you can." I yell soon as the bullets start flying towards us.

I hear my men returning fire as we advance towards the entrances, shooting down any of the assholes standing guard from the top balconies.

I'm just getting to the sliding glass door when I feel a sting in my arm right as the glass shatters in front of me. Looking down, I see that a bullet has grazed me. Ignoring it, I step inside.

As I'm coming further into the room, movement on my right catches my eye but not before bullets are yet again flying at my head.

I duck and roll, coming back up and taking my shot before I even can see the fucker clearly. I take great pleasure however, as I watch his eyes roll to the back of his head from the shot I put between his eyes.

"Stupid fuck!" I say out loud, reaching the landing on the stairs where he was at.

A movement behind me has me turning around quickly, my gun at the ready.

"It's just me." Grim says before I can shoot him.

"Don't sneak up on me." I growl back.

"Bottom floor, clear." I hear Tanker say through coms. "Going to the basement."

"Be careful." I reply back.

Grim and I make our way up the stairs slowly. I'm glad to have him at my back.

As we get to the top and look down the hallway, there's three doors on each side.

"One at a time. Take turns covering." I whisper to him and he gives a nod in return.

Getting to the first door, I kick it in as he rushes inside but it's completely empty except for a bed in the middle of the room.

I can feel my heart beat rushing through my ears as I notice the bed has restraints attached at all the corners as well as in the middle.

Backing out, we continue to the next room but we find the same thing there as well. Behind every door, it's the same.

"Fuck! What were they doing? Loaning them out?" Grim growls in disgust.

"Top floor, clear. Tanker? How are you guys doing?" I say over coms.

I start to worry when he doesn't immediately answer.

"Penned down at the basement entrance behind the house. Ranger's been hit, I can't see how bad. Gando and his men are tending to him. See if you two can find the entrance from inside. Take these fucks from both directions!"

He finally says back through the crackling sounds.

"On our way." Tanker says immediately and we turn back to the stairs.

Making our way back to the lower floor, we look for a door that we haven't already previously checked.

That's when we find the pantry closet in the kitchen with another solid door behind it.

"Found it. We will need to blow it." Tanker watches our backs as I kneel down to pull out some explosives from my backpack.

Working quickly, I get it rigged up and we move farther away into the house behind another wall.

Using my cell, I press a button and the entire house shakes as the door flies inward into the basement.

Rushing to the door, bullets fly at us. It's a bad place to try to get a bead on the fucks in that hallway.

Hunkering back down on either side of the pantry door, we let the stupid fucks continue to fire. Hopefully they are close to running out of ammo.

"When their shots slow down Grim, we all shoot at the same time. They can't protect their backs at the same time they protect their front." I say with a grin.

"Got it!" Grim answers through coms.

"Why are you smiling?" Tanker asks.

"This is fun. Aren't you having fun?" I smile widely back at him.

"You are seriously fucked up in the head brother." He shakes his head but smiles back anyway.

We wait several long minutes before their shots slow way down. We can hear them talking, probably thinking they killed us all. My smile grows.

"Everyone ready? Go!" I shout and we all turn up the heat on the fucks in that hallway.

The ones trying to get further away from Grim's shots put themselves directly in front of mine and Tanker's sights. Poor fucks didn't stand a chance.

"I don't see any more movement on my end." Grim says.

"We don't see any here either. Proceed with caution though." Tanker says as he and I descend the stairs into the basement.

Looking around, there's around ten men lying on the floor, bleeding out. There's a few doors on one side of the hallway and I'm betting there's girls behind them.

"Let's get these doors open. Be careful though, a few of the fuckers may have hidden themselves inside." I command.

Grim makes quick work of the first door. We slowly open it, looking inside. There's at least five females inside all of which look scared.

"Tanker, see if any of them speak English. Try to get them to understand we are the good guys." I whisper to him afraid a loud voice may set them to screaming.

Grim and I move to the second door to get it open. This time as soon as it swings inward, bullets start flying out.

The stupid bastard must not have had very many bullets though because after the first three shots, I hear the gun click on empty chamber.

I walk through the door with a smile but it falters when I lay eyes on a face that I never thought I would see again.

Standing in a far corner with two other girls is my sister Melody. Her eyes are the only indication that she recognizes me although she says nothing.

Looking back at the fucker between us with his slicked back hair and all his jewelry I'm pretty sure of who he is.

"Peter, I assume?" I snarl in his direction.

His eyes look wide and I see the second that he decides to make a grab for the girls but a shot rings out behind me.

I watch as Peter falls to the floor with a single gunshot wound to the head. Quickly looking behind me, I see Ranger leaning against the door with his hand holding his stomach which is covered in blood. Unable to hold himself up any longer, he slides down the wall to the floor.

Running over to him, I check for a pulse which I find to be barely there.

"Just make sure I make it back home brother." He whispers one last time before he breathes his last.

"Fuck!" I grit out.

Standing up, I look back at both Tanker and Grim who look just as sad as I do.

"I'll go see if I can find a vehicle. We'll need it for the women anyway." Grim says quickly before striding away.

Looking back at Melody, my heart aches as she makes no move to come closer to me.

"Mel? It's okay now." I whisper softly, moving closer.

She watches me as if she sees a ghost and doesn't comprehend what is currently happening. As I get closer, her eyes widen, never leaving my face.

Reaching my hand out, I touch her arm and that's when she collapses, tears streaming down her face.

"I thought I'd never see you again." She whispers through her tears and I wrap her in my arms.

"I'd have been here sooner but I thought you were dead Mel. I'm so sorry." I hold her tightly to me.

"We should go before the locals get here." Grim says quickly.

"The police here are in on it. I'll help get the girls. They trust me." Melody says, standing up.

"Well let's get the fuck out of here. I'm ready to go home!" Tanker announces loudly, then looks contrite as the other two girls still in this room shrink further back. "Sorry." He holds his hands out, then drops them to his sides.

Melody walks over to them, talking softly. I'm not sure what she says to them but they straighten their spines, walking towards the door.

She rounds up the others from the room next door, getting them all loaded into the two SUV's that Grim hotwired.

We offer Gando and his men a lift back down to the town but they refuse the offer. They say goodbye to us instead just outside the perimeter of the property before disappearing into the woods.

On our way to the plane that is waiting for us, I make a quick call to Skeeter so that he can get our FBI friends to make sure we aren't held up because of the women not having identification.

Only one of the women is not a natural born United States citizen but when given the choice, she chose to go with us back to New Orleans.

Our contacts will give her all the papers that she needs so that she never has to worry about being deported.

Today has been a great day. I think to myself as I watch my sister talk to the other women on the plane.

She seems to be taking everything so well but I know she will need help in the months to come. I still don't know what kind of hell she endured while being a captive.

My mind thinks back to those beds with the chains and I shiver.

No matter what, I will make certain that she gets fully healed from all of it.

Chapter 10
Buzz

The last four weeks have gone by slowly with getting Melody back into a routine and getting the other girls set-up at safe houses as well.

Since we don't know who the head of the snake is with the trafficking ring, we all thought it best to place all the new girls in areas that only a very few of us know about.

Getting back to New Orleans we learned from Skeeter that several more of the other girls are missing.

We're on the hunt for the traitor that has infiltrated our club. Skeeter is currently devising a plan to draw the fucker out. Those few of us that are in the know can't wait to fillet the skin from his fucking body.

Ranger's funeral was held the first Saturday after our return. It's been the only time I've seen any emotions from my sister since the day we rescued her.

Although I've arranged for a doctor to be with the girls in their location, she's yet to open up about the things she went through.

I know it could take time but from being in the military, I know a lot about post traumatic stress.

I'd much rather she be a screaming, crying mess than the type that keeps it all bottled inside. Holding that shit in will eat you up until nothing is left.

Now that I have her back, I won't allow anything to take control of her mind and take her away from me again.

I need that sweet smartass bubbly girl back. The only one who's never been afraid to tell me to fuck off.

I've texted with Markayla a lot since being back. I could tell she was excited for me to have found my sister again. It was all thanks to her.

Those first few weeks, we talked about all kinds of things. I even learned her love of strawberry milkshakes made with real fresh strawberries. Not those that come in a can.

The last few times I've messaged her though, she's taken longer to answer and it's always one word answers which is starting to piss me off.

This is why I've contacted her father, Tony who has informed me that she's been talking to some guy that works in the town they are currently staying in.

That shit ain't going to fly. She's mine and it's time that she realizes that. I'm sure it would help if I told her how I felt. I've never been good at putting that shit into words.

I'll be damned if I sit back while some yuppie in Colorado takes her from me though. I'll run him over with my fucking bike first!

———

Sitting here at my computer in the silence of my loft a plan begins to form in my mind. I can't stop the shit eating grin from my face as the plan comes completely together in my head.

It'll surely piss Markayla off which could make things a little more fun.

The thought of her eyes shooting fire at me has me rock hard in seconds.

Oh, yes. I want that so badly.

Picking up my phone, I dial Baratta and he answers on the second ring.

"I have a plan and you're going to help me with it." I say into the phone.

"About time." He laughs back.

As I explain my plan in further detail, he laughs even harder.

I can't wait to put it all in motion.

Markayla

"Hey, I'm going out with my new friends from town tonight. I should be back before midnight." I say to my parents while grabbing my purse and keys to one of the cars.

Here lately, it seems to be all that I do. Go out with some of the friends that I've made in town.

We usually go to the local bar. It's small but they have a live band and their drinks aren't that bad.

Looking back at my parents to see if they heard me, I see them smiling at each other as if they have a secret.

"You guys okay?" I ask.

"Yep. You go and have fun with your friends." My father says way too cheerfully.

Thinking that it may be because the two of them are looking forward to being alone, I shake my head to clear the thoughts of them being intimate.

"See you later. Love you guys!" I yell, heading out the door.

I pull up to the bar about ten minutes later. Looking around I see that they are packed which is nothing surprising since they are the only bar within a fifty mile radius.

Spotting Wills jeep parked in the second row, I know that the rest of my friends are already inside. So I head towards the door.

The inside is dimly lit with the music blaring through the speakers and people dancing everywhere.

I finally spot my friends on the other side of the room at a table talking and laughing.

"Hey guys!" I say, taking a seat.

"Markayla! You're finally here. I just ordered you a drink, it should be here in a few minutes." Will smiles at me from across the table.

Looking at my friend, I just don't understand how anyone could name their daughter William.

She told me it was because her parents had only picked out boy names while her momma was pregnant with her.

Her mom thought it was a brilliant idea so after Will was born and she had two more girls, she named both of them boy names too.

I never explained to my parents that they were women and not men.

"You need to catch up with these other two Markayla." Adrian says from the end of the table. "They both gulped down two beers before you got here."

"It was Charlie's idea to see who can drink the fastest." Will replies with a shrug.

"Oh holy fucking hotness. Who the hell is that? I want some!" Adrian says huskily.

Looking at her, the rest of us follow her eyes to see what she's looking at and I begin to laugh as my eyes meet the guy's in question.

He half grins as he heads in our direction.

"Do you know him?" Charlie whispers to me quickly.

"Yeah. That's my cousin Alessandro." I answer.

"Fuck. I want a cousin like him." Will murmurs looking up at Alessandro.

"What are you doing here?" I ask him.

"I came to help a friend find something he lost." He looks behind him and that's when I see Buzz walking across the room.

All of the air leaves my lungs as my eyes eat him up.

"Another cousin?" Will leans over to ask with hope in her eyes.

"Definitely not a cousin." I whisper back, not taking my eyes from Buzz.

A slow song begins to play in the background and the dancers' movements slow on the dance floor.

When Buzz reaches my side, he doesn't say a word as he grabs my hand pulling me from my chair.

We make our way to the dance floor and he pulls me tightly against him as we begin to sway to the music.

"Your parents said you were out with your friend Will. Where is he?" I half growls in my ear.

Chill bumps are crawling up my arms from having him so close to me and an ache begins deep within my core.

It takes me several seconds to realize what he said and I can't stop the giggle that escapes.

"You think this is funny Markayla?" He growls again.

"Actually yes." I answer honestly.

Knowing that he's jealous of the thought that I would be with a man makes me feel all kinds of things.

"Where is he?" He asks seriously.

"She...she is at the table you just pulled me from." I answer, trying to smooth his clenched jaw.

"She?" He looks into my eyes questioningly.

"Yep. William, Charlie and Adrian. They are sisters that have a mom with a wicked sense of humor." I smile back at him brightly as his muscles that were so tense a few minutes ago begin to relax.

He lays his forehead against my own, continuing to sway with the music.

"Your dad made it sound like you were out with guys." He pulls back with a grin.

"I never explained to him that they were females." I shrug.

"I'm beginning to think you did that on purpose. You knew I would find out." He looks into my eyes again.

"Maybe." Looking back up at him, he slams his mouth down on my own.

Thank God the music is so loud. If it wasn't, everyone in this bar would hear my moans.

"I'm taking you back with me." He states after breaking off the kiss.

"Don't I get a say in this?" I pull back with a serious look that I don't actually mean.

"Nope." He says, never cracking a smile. "You will either walk out of this bar with me on your own or I will carry you out."

"Hmm. Those are my choices?" I ask, turning my head to the side as if to think it over.

"Don't push me Markayla." He growls and I love it.

"Then carry me out of here big boy." I whisper back, leaning forward as I do knowing it'll give him a peak at the top of my breasts down my shirt.

He growls low when his eyes notice.

Next thing I know, I'm thrown over his shoulder with his hand delivering a slap to my ass. I laugh the whole way out of the bar.

Buzz

Getting Markayla back to the room I rented for the night at a hotel, I don't give her even a second to look around the room when I have her pressed against the wall.

Pressing my hardness into her backside, I kiss and suck on the side of her neck. I hope I leave marks for everyone to see that she is mine.

"I'm going to fuck you against this wall until you scream my name and then I'm going to do it again in that bed over there. I've been without you too long." I grit my teeth together, trying to not hurt her with the passion I feel for only her.

"Yes. I want that too." She whispers back.

I reach down quickly, undoing her jeans, shoving them as far as I can down her legs. My own only gets as far as the top of my thighs when my hard cock springs free.

Putting myself between her legs, I coat myself in her wetness.

"Always so wet for me babe." I whisper through the torture as I glide back and forth.

Lining up my shaft with her center, I slam fully inside of her. Both of us, moaning at the same time.

Unable to take it slow, I become a jackhammer as I pull nearly out and back in over and over again.

I feel her insides as they begin to throb indicating that she's close to coming. Speeding up my pace so that I will come with her, we both rush over that edge until we are spent.

I've never come so hard in my life and that's when I realize that my stupid ass forgot the condom in my pants pocket.

"Fuck babe, I forgot a condom." I say apologetically as I watch my come slowly leak down her thighs.

"I'm on the pill." She smiles back at me.

"So I can keep going bare?" I ask with hope in my voice.

"Yes." She answers.

"Thank fuck! Because that was the best thing I've ever felt in my life!" I exclaim, picking her up into my arms to place her in the bed.

"What are you doing?" She asks sleepily.

"It's time for round two. I told you what I had planned." I answer seriously and she begins to giggle at me.

Her giggles don't last long before they turn into moans.

I look forward to our future together. I'll always make sure she's protected just like I will for my sister.

The End…For Now

Skeeter
Night Howler's MC
New Orleans, Book 2

Katrina: oblivious, fearful, gutsy
Skeeter: vexed, steadfast, indomitable

After meeting with the Feds, Skeeter finds out some of the women that his crew rescued from the human traffickers has started disappearing and only his crew knew where the women were. With a traitor in his mists, Skeeter must flush him out and save these women.

Katrina suffers from complete amnesia, not knowing her real name or her own age. The only people she knows and trusts are the men who rescued her and the other women. One day one of her rescuers comes to her door and tells her she needs to come with him.

Trusting these men, she willing goes only to find herself taken back into a situation she had hoped had ended for good. Determined not to be a victim again, Katrina starts looking for a way to escape, fearing the worst and thinking the Night Howlers are the bad guys now. This madman says Katrina belongs to him.

What would happen if she tries to escape and he catches her? Skeeter doesn't know who he can trust among his own men and has to find these women in time before they are sold or worse.

Who would dare become a traitor to the Night Howlers?
Can Skeeter figure out who the traitor is and who he can trust?
Can he rescue Katrina and the other women in time?

GET IT HERE:
https://books2read.com/Skeeter

Bear's Saviour
Wolfsbane Ridge MC, Book 5

Sara: sharp, responsible, determined
Bear: mature, powerful, repentant

While taking time away from her studies to be a nurse to help her family's business, Sara Blackcat meets and falls for an older man. She and Bear spend one glorious night together, but Bear regrets it thinking he's too old for the younger woman. She's determined to show him love knows no number.

With only a few days left until graduation and completing her dream of becoming a registered nurse, Sara is working a clinical shift at the local hospital when a man comes in brandishing a firearm. Sara manages to send a text before the gunman confiscates all the phones.

When the Wolfsbane Ridge MC finds out what is going on, they jump to action. The people and town are theirs to protect. Bear becomes fiercely protective when he finds out Sara is in the hospital in the hands of this madman.

Will he reach her in time to save her?

Will he realize how he really feels about her, that love knows no age?

GET IT HERE: https://books2read.com/BearsSaviour

Torque's Gaze
Wolfsbane Ridge MC, Book 6

Jesse: astute, charming, statuesque
Torque: serious, ethereal, reticent

Brutus, Torque's rescued stray and town legend, suddenly falls ill. Torque needs the town's only vet, Jesse Rayne, immediately. Her help is the only way to save his beloved dog. But no one knows where she is and the last time anyone saw her was when she left for a ride out at Hayden's ranch.

When Romeo, the gelding that Jesse was last seen riding, returns to the ranch without Jesse, the search begins to find her. Torque sets out knowing time may be short for Brutus as he only seems to get sicker. When he finds Jesse, she has hit her head and wakes up looking into his piercing light colored eyes thinking she's died and is in heaven staring into the eyes of an angel.

On the way back to town, Torque tells Jesse about Brutus and they rush to the vet clinic to try to save him. Realizing there is a pattern and other animals are coming down with the same symptoms, Jesse confides in Torque.

Can the two of them figure out who is poisoning animals in White Summer?

Or will they also become victims of this psychopath?

GET IT HERE:
https://books2read.com/TorquesGaze

Arin's Light
Poison Pen, Book 3

After spending seven years living in the shadows, Arin Conelly has a chance to shine. Will she take it?

Giving up her baby for adoption when she was 15 years old seemed like the hardest decision Arin ever had to make. Looking into her baby's bright eyes, Arin knew she was doing the right thing.

Now seven years later she is faced with another tough decision. Should she stay in the town where she grew up, always living in the shadow of her famous bosses or can she make a name for herself?

During his law internship, Taylor Burns' mentor became ill during a high profile case. A case he was losing. Taylor stepped up, winning the case and the notoriety that came with it. Since then he has specialized in family law, with a few exceptions. Poison Pen is one of those exceptions.

He came to White Summer to help on a custody case. But it has become his third home. The first being Alaska, the second the courtroom.

Something about the town and the people in it keeps pulling him back.

It couldn't possibly be the hazel eyed beauty he can't keep his eyes or his thoughts off of at Poison Pen. Could it?

GET IT HERE:
https://books2read.com/ArinsLight

**Reaper's Jewels
Night Howler's MC Book 1**

Reaper- regretful, apologetic and determined.

Jade- rejected, angry and betrayed.

He regrets letting her go.

She refused to be somewhere she's not wanted.
So she left, had Reaper's child in secret, and
raised her on her own. She never wants her
daughter to feel the rejection she felt all those
years ago.

Reaper must learn how to be a father.

Jade must learn how to forgive.

Is this a love that can be saved? Can they come
together as a family? Or will Reaper lose
everything because he chose the wrong woman
all those years ago?

This Series has ties to the Wolfsbane Ridge MC
Series by the same Author. Can be read as a
stand alone but it is highly recommended to
read the Wolfsbane Ridge MC Series first.
GET IT HERE:
https://books2read.com/ReapersJewels

Timber's Fairy
Wolfsbane Ridge MC Book 1

Mina: beautiful, smart, innocent and troubled.
Timber: tall, dark and dangerous.

A flame filled passion burns hot between them
from their very first meeting.

But Mina has a past.

From creepy text messages and rose petals on
the front porch, to exploding trucks. Someone is
out to get her.

Timber, President of Wolfsbane MC, is a
dangerous man. He will stop at nothing to
protect his club and the woman he's falling for.

But will he be able to get to her in time? If not,
she could suffer a fate worse than death.

She never wanted to fall for a biker.

He never wanted an Old Lady.

But now they need each other, more than they'll
ever know.

"Until you tell me that you are mine and that
you are willing to give us a chance, I plan to

keep you in a constant state of arousal so that you understand how you make me feel all the time. But the minute you say you are mine, Mina, I plan to bring you to this room and make you scream my name so many times you lose your voice."

GET IT HERE:

https://books2read.com/TimbersFairy

About The Author
Marissa Ann

Marissa Ann grew up in two very different worlds, the big city and the rural South. Mobile Alabama offered her the opportunities to not only see other cultures but to experience them as well.

Every weekend she spent most of her time on the beach of Perdido with her dog, Buddy. It didn't matter what time of the day, even midnight, they could be found walking along the shore in search of seashells.

Buddy passed away in 1997 and she still misses him today. You never forget your true best friends, even the four legged ones.

When she wasn't in Alabama with her dad, she was in North Mississippi with her mom. Mostly spending time with her Grandfather who taught her not only how to grow a garden but how to completely live off the land as well as to love animals.

Today, she spends her time in rural North Mississippi with her husband, the kids and all of their animals on a hobby farm.

She always said she would write books one day even though many thought she never would. She made a promise to a childhood friend who left this world for the next in 2015. That she would finally write and publish at least one.

Her first book hit the market in 2018 and she's never looked back. She now has several out with many more scheduled for release.

Book 2 Skeeter
https://books2read.com/Skeeter

Poison Pen Series
Book 1 Baratta's Darkness
https://books2read.com/BarattasDarkness

Book 2 Lily's Shadow
https://books2read.com/LilysShadow

Book 3 Arin's Light
https://books2read.com/ArinsLight

A Call Of Magic Limited Edition featuring
Hydra: The Dragon Keeper
https://books2read.com/callofmagic

Let's Play, A Limited Edition Sports Romance
Collection featuring:
All I've Got
https://books2read.com/letsplay

Sea's Of Rissa, a Collection of Poems
https://books2read.com/seasofrissa

Sign Up for Marissa Ann's Newsletter
https://mailchi.mp/3ca12e9bcaec/1ex5ytjtmd